ASE BASE BASE **BASE** BASE

MP CAMP CAMP **CAMP** CA

M FREEDOM **FREEDOM** FR

BASE CAMP FREEDOM

Joe East

iUniverse, Inc.
Bloomington

Base Camp Freedom

iUniverse books may be ordered through booksellers or by contacting:

iUniverse
1663 Liberty Drive
Bloomington, IN 47403
www.iuniverse.com
1-800-Authors (1-800-288-4677)

ISBN: 978-1-4759-3474-8 (sc)
ISBN: 978-1-4759-3476-2 (hc)
ISBN: 978-1-4759-3475-5 (e)

Printed in the United States of America

iUniverse rev. date: 7/2/2012

Contents

Prologue

Lewis fired his automatic pistol as he burst into the communications room. It was unbelievable—four dead marines lay at his feet. Before he could access the navigation computer, he felt a crushing blow against his back. As Lewis sank to the floor, everything grew blurry and sounds became indistinct.

"Hey, Sarge, five are down in the commo room—four are good guys!"

"Watson, secure the area. Nobody else goes in until the Lieutenant says it's okay."

"Wilco."

First Sergeant Barnett keyed his mic to the command frequency. "Lieutenant, we've shut down the terrorists in this section—three dead and three prisoners. Sir, we lost four marines."

"Okay, First Sergeant. We're clearing up our section. No marine casualties here but two bad guys down and some equipment damage. I'll be there as soon as I post guards."

The year is 2150. The political landscape of our world has changed greatly, especially since the middle of the twenty-first century.

In 2090 the United States, Canada, and Mexico merged into one country for their common survival. Our new nation was named the United American Republic (UAR).

Other nations also consolidated their governments and territories. Geopolitical consolidation was the best defense against the enormous economic, political, and military power held by mega-corporations.

Smaller countries were at the mercy of these large corporations. The best example is Africa. A large African-based corporation named Transvaal bought the African continent one country at a time. Transvaal developed a winning strategy of underwriting simultaneous revolutions in several countries. After the weakened governments failed, Transvaal would establish puppet governments whose very existence was owned and controlled by Transvaal's board of directors.

The United Nations, never a unified or credible force was incapable of stopping simultaneous national revolutions.

Since the beginning of reliable and efficient space travel and the discovery of unlimited mineral wealth in the asteroid belt, the UAR and Transvaal have been engaged in space-based mining operations. Minerals mined in space are shipped back to Earth and sold for huge profits.

To protect its investment, the UAR established a special unit within its military called the Space Marines. As military units go, Space Marines is a very small organization and is totally funded by UAR mining contractors. It is limited to two hundred fifty members because any military force equates to overhead and cuts into profits. Maintaining the Space Marines is like owning a very expensive insurance policy—each year you pay a hefty premium while hoping the policy is never needed. One half of the force is deployed and the other half remains Earth side, undergoing team rebuilding, training, and taking much-deserved leave. Not surprising, turnover is high.

The Space Marines' sole mission is to protect the United American Republic's space station, transport, and mining operations run by UAR contractors.

This story is about the members of a marine unit assigned to Moon Base Freedom.

CHAPTER 1
Basic Training

My skin felt like a battleground where sand fleas and horseflies were fighting for supremacy. Sweat-drenched and tired, I lay on the ground beside the others, panting for breath in temperatures exceeding 106 degrees.

Sergeant Rafael Hernandez, our devoted drill sergeant, walked up and down our rest area, never hesitating in his critique of our latest performance. According to Drill Sergeant Hernandez, we were undoubtedly "the worst bunch of recruits it was his displeasure to meet." He further intoned that someone at Fort Sonora must be "out to get him" by saddling him with such a misbegotten bunch of maggots. I now fully realize why recruiters skip the interesting parts of basic training during their recruitment spiel. If a young person only knew what was about to happen to him, our government would have to resurrect the draft!

Looking over at my buddies, I almost smiled. Laura Smith was picking a cactus spine from John Rafferty's back while Brenda Chan was brushing sand from Smith's shoulder. It kinda reminded me of an old nature film showing monkeys grooming one another. But hey, I'm not making light of this situation; we take care of one another. It's the only way to make it through basic. I'm certain that basic trainees were the ones who coined the phrase "cooperate and graduate." Pity the loner who can't or won't rely on anyone at any time. A helping hand during an obstacle course (run for the second time because we "lacked enthusiasm" during the first run), a bunkmate washing your uniform for an inspection tomorrow morning while you are on guard duty are but examples of situations where a buddy can save your ass.

We were completing our final three-day exercise, three days of long marches interspersed with simulated attacks by fiendishly clever aggressor forces, and sandwiched between sleep measured in minutes—not hours. The bastards acted like they knew our route-of-march beforehand. Knowing Drill Sergeant Hernandez, I'm sure they did.

The desert terrain defies description. While most of the terrain is flat, there are small hills and arroyos in our maneuver area. The vegetation consists of an abundance of cacti, including the saguaro, prickly pear, cholla, staghorn, organ-pipe, and barrel cactus. Additional indigenous plants include the creosote bush, burro bush, mesquite, palo verde, Joshua tree, and ironwood. It never rained during my twelve weeks of basic training. What a hellhole.

In these final days before completing basic training, I sometimes think of what I would be doing had I not chosen to join the marines. Attending college was impossible because the cost was prohibitive and my parents are not wealthy. I could have become a farm or factory worker for one of the corporations. They had jobs available but only offered minimum wages since unskilled labor was so plentiful. No, that was not for me. Besides, I wanted adventure!

My name is Jim Hawkins. I'm from a small Mississippi town in the United American Republic (UAR). It seems that my whole life was spent preparing for a military career. I played sports throughout school and excelled in advanced mathematics, computer applications, and science. After graduation most of my classmates had chosen to work at either the local food-processing factory or the corporate farm. The same corporation, Chickasaw Food, owned both. They were given an apartment, a credit account, and free access to public transportation. Several had even married. Although they were only paid a minimum wage, it was not a bad life. The company provided free medical care and a two-week vacation at one of their resort properties.

A couple of my classmates were from wealthy families and were able to attend college. Their futures were assured—the wealthy class would continue.

Because I came from the working class, my career choices were limited. I didn't want to spend the rest of my life working in a factory six days a week doing the same thing over and over. In any case, I chose a military career because of the travel and adventure promised by a military recruiter. At this moment, I hated that damn recruiter.

My mother and father disapproved of my enlisting in the marines. They were afraid for me, especially after hearing news about the UAR being involved in periodic fighting with Transvaal. At this moment, sweating in the Sonoran Desert, I wished I had listened to them.

"All right, people, since you're done with your naps, *off and on*!" This quaint expression really means "Get off your butts and on your feet!" As a unit, we rose and achieved a platoon formation with a quickness learned by countless repetition. No sense in making Sergeant Hernandez mad; he could be a real bastard if you pissed him off.

Back at the barracks, we cleaned up and got ready for a trip to the mess hall. There's one thing I can say about military food. Someone must be making a huge profit by selling this stuff to the military! We often joke about how tasteless the food is, but maybe that's for the best. The cooks slinging the food on our trays did not appear to be qualified for jobs in any commercial restaurant.

"Hey, Hawkins, how did you miss seeing the last ambush? You were on point and led the whole platoon into a wicked crossfire. My body is still sore from the training rounds!"

I looked over at Stevens and quietly retorted, "Well, since I'm not Superman, I guess being without sleep for more than forty-eight hours must have affected my sight, you asshole!"

"If I wasn't so tired, I would whip your sorry ass."

"Oh yeah? You and who else?"

At that time, Sagura stepped between us and said, "If you two don't shut up, I'll be the one whipping ass around here."

That stopped the argument. We both knew that Private Angel Sagura could stomp our butts—singly or together. She held a second-degree black belt in karate and had become the most feared and respected opponent in hand-to-hand training classes. Even Corporal Ramos, our assistant DI, steered clear of her.

After chow I looked at the duty roster and found that I had

drawn barracks watch from midnight until 0500. *That's just great!* I thought as I fell asleep. Only four hours of sleep after a three-day exercise. How lucky can a guy be?

At 2355, Stevens shook my shoulder and said, "Okay, Hawkins, your turn." It took me only three and a half minutes to dress and grab my weapon. After formally relieving Stevens, I began walking my post.

Walking around the barracks, I noticed the usual things. Everything was in its place. Garbage cans neatly placed on a concrete pad, mops and brooms hanging in their rack, and our platoon flag in its holder. Except for occasional wild animal noises, it was quiet and the air was several degrees cooler than inside the barracks.

Around 0230 I heard footsteps. As I turned toward the intruder and gave the challenge, a quiet voice said, "At ease, Private Hawkins."

I kept my weapon on the intruder as he slowly moved under one of the outside lights. I asked him the password, to which he responded correctly. Afterward he introduced himself as Captain Morris Whittaker.

Brass! We didn't see many officers during basic training. I was thinking, *This officer knows my name. What have I done now?*

Captain Whittaker said, "Private Hawkins, I was out walking tonight and thought I would stop by my old barracks and reminisce."

"How do you know my name, sir?"

"I stopped by the orderly room and saw your name on the guard duty roster."

Before I could fully digest that explanation, Captain Whittaker added, "I want to congratulate you on completing a very difficult part of your life. Getting through basic without any major problems is quite an accomplishment."

"Thank you, sir."

He continued. "Sometimes I miss basic. I made a lot of friends during my twelve-week stint and have some great memories of those days." He looked me in the eye and added, "There's not enough money in the free world to get me to go through that again!"

We both laughed quietly at that.

During the next twenty minutes or so, Captain Whittaker asked me a bunch of questions about my family, friends, and my impression of the marines. I didn't mind answering his questions because I felt that we had a lot in common and because guard duty is a boring job. It was nice having someone to talk to. After he left the area, the remaining time on duty didn't seem so long.

Only two days until graduation! Everybody in the platoon is extremely anxious about which assignment we will draw after graduating boot camp. The rumors abound and range from a posting at boot camp as a permanent party, assignment to one of the UAR carrier forces, to embassy duty in a foreign country. It's all we can talk about. Fortunately for us, Sergeant Hernandez and corporals Ramos and Turner have eased up on harassing us unless someone does something really stupid.

Tomorrow is graduation. I have mixed emotions as we scrub our barracks a final time. I began thinking back to my first day in the marines.

I vividly remember the chartered air-conditioned bus driving through the imposing gates of Fort Sonora in northern Mexico. Fort Sonora is the basic training site of the UAR Marine Corps. I was among forty recruits riding on this particular bus. Early that morning we arrived at the airport in Phoenix, Arizona. We were met by a marine sergeant who checked off our names on a roster. He gave us a sack lunch and a booklet about the marines and led us to the bus for the ride to Fort Sonora. It was a long and uneventful trip. After skimming through the booklet, I noted that a squad is made up of ten marines and a platoon consists of four squads. The rank structure was relatively simple—I was a private, the lowest rank in the marines! Beyond private was corporal, sergeant, lieutenant, captain, major, colonel, and general.

One page caught my attention. It was a description of an elite marine unit named space marines. These marines were responsible for guarding our launch facilities, space station and mining operation on the moon. Only a few marines were chosen for this unique assignment. I read that page several times. Unlike other marine specialties listed in the booklet, there was no information about how to volunteer.

After entering the fort, our bus drove along a main thoroughfare lined with palm trees. Eventually we arrived at a large concrete parking lot near a white single-story building.

The bus stopped and the door opened. A lone figure dressed in a tan uniform strode to the entrance of the bus and slowly scanned each person. "*Get off my bus, you maggots!*" the sergeant screamed.

A stampede of startled faces leaped to their feet and pushed one another as we attempted to rush from the bus as one. Welcome to basic training.

As we piled off the bus, the oppressive desert heat hit me like a blast furnace. A blinding afternoon sun made me squint as the sergeant began screaming for us to line up. The recruiter had failed to mention this little detail about basic training. I began to wonder what else had been omitted.

Once we were assembled into what passed as a platoon formation, the sergeant started us toward our future as the newest additions to the marines. "Listen up! My name is Drill Sergeant Rafael Hernandez. I have the misfortune to have been assigned to take you through the next twelve weeks of basic training and make you into marines. During the upcoming twelve weeks, I'm going to be your momma and your daddy. You won't get out of basic training unless you have satisfied me that you are capable of becoming marines. From now on, I will tell you what to do, when to do it, and how to do it. Your only job is to follow orders.

"As an introduction to your new life, you people are going to learn how to march. The first thing you will learn is how to stand at attention. When you hear the command, '*tenshun,*' you are to bring your heels together at an approximate forty-five degree angle, stand tall, hands cupped by your side, thumbs pointed along the seams of your trousers, chest out, head straight, and eyes forward." Sergeant Hernandez demonstrated the position of "tenshun" for us. "There is no talking in ranks! Do you understand?"

Startled, some of us said, "Yes, sir."

"What did you maggots say? I can't hear you!"

With a lot more enthusiasm, we all roared, *"Yes, sir!"*

"That's better. Now pay attention. *Platoon, tenshun!"*

As a unit, we came to the position of attention. Unfortunately, it was not to our drill sergeant's satisfaction. He walked by each of us rapping us on the offending portion of our bodies with a short stick he carried until he was satisfied all of us finally understood this simple command.

One of the recruits seemed to think this was funny. He was standing next to me and somewhat at attention with a big grin on his face when Sergeant Hernandez noticed him grinning. Two steps and four seconds later, Sergeant Hernandez swung his stick and the once-grinning recruit had a red weal on his face and tears streaming down his cheeks.

Ooooh, that's gotta hurt! I could feel the wind as the stick whizzed past my face.

Sergeant Hernandez got in the recruit's face and screamed, *"Do you still think this is funny, maggot?"*

The recruit blurted, *"No, sir!"*

Sergeant Hernandez went to the front of the formation and said, "You people better remember what I said. I will tell you what to do, when to do it, and how to do it. And I don't remember telling you to grin."

Sweat began running down my back and into my eyes. It sure was hot! Cautiously cutting my eyes to one side, I noticed others were sweating too.

After a lengthy period of marching back and forth on the hot concrete parking lot and learning the rudiments of *column left,* and *column right,* we were dismissed and sent into the white building. Inside, the air conditioning felt like heaven.

We were directed to a long counter and given a duffel bag, three pair of pants, web belt, three shirts, six sets of underwear, two towels, six pair of socks and two caps. On our side of the counter Sergeant Hernandez was yelling at us to put our things in our duffel bags and move out. I had an uneasy feeling that he would never be satisfied with our performance.

Further down the counter we were issued a backpack, a small shovel, canteen, hunting knife, lightweight sleeping bag, mosquito net, nylon rope, and first-aid kit. We were told to take everything with us and not let it out of our sight.

After the barbershop was the medical office. A team of white-suited men and women ordered us to strip naked and line up in four rows. We received numerous shots. They were given to us in both arms and buttocks. I felt like a pincushion after passing the gauntlet of medical technicians administering shots. Afterward we were allowed to put on our military-issued underwear. Nobody seemed to have the time or inclination to stare at one another.

Our final stop in the medical office was to sit in a chair similar to the ones found in a dentist's office. Shortly afterward a doctor came and cut a small incision in my forearm and inserted a computer chip. He said, "This is where your military history will be recorded. It will contain your complete records including medical history, pay, and a lot of other data. A duplicate of all entries will be maintained at marine headquarters." I was told I would never even notice the chip in my arm.

After this ordeal, we were sent to another room where we were told to dress in our military clothing. Finally we entered a room where we were issued boots. Although our clothing was baggy and the trousers had to be held up by the web belt, the boots were carefully fitted.

Outside the building Sergeant Hernandez directed us into waiting trucks that drove us to our barracks at the far end of the base. It was almost dark when we arrived. Sweat was soaking through my new uniform.

The barracks were sparsely furnished, dimly lit, and without air conditioning. Gray metal beds were aligned in two rows. The beds contained nothing more than a six-centimeter mattress. Behind each bed was a gray metal locker. Inside the locker door was a diagram showing us how to arrange our clothing and gear. Each locker also contained a bucket with a scrub brush, laundry soap, bath soap, disposable razors, toothbrush, and toothpaste.

Nobody spoke or had any inclination to speak. We were all tired and miserable and wondering what we had gotten ourselves into. Sergeant Hernandez told us we had missed dinner but would get to sleep in.

After he left, I immediately stretched out on my bunk and fell asleep. I guess the others did too. We didn't realize 5:00 a.m. (0500 military time) was Sergeant Hernandez's version of "sleeping in!"

At 0500 we met the other members of our "cadre," Corporal Joyce Turner and Corporal Philip Ramos. These non-commissioned officers were like clones of Sergeant Hernandez. At least one cadre member was with us all day every day for the duration of basic training.

Corporal Turner was a tall, muscular blonde woman who looked and acted like she could take care of herself in any situation. She demonstrated her fighting ability on several occasions during basic training.

Corporal Ramos was a short, skinny man with the disposition of a junkyard dog. He delighted in getting a foolish recruit to "take the first swing." After two such incidents, nobody was stupid enough to try again.

"*Hit the deck, maggots!* Today is the first day of your life as a marine. What the hell do you think this is—a rest home?"

Bunks containing the slow movers were overturned, and all of us scrambled to get dressed as if the barracks was on fire. Needless to say it wasn't fast enough and we had to repeat this procedure until we were exhausted.

We marched to the mess hall and were rushed through the chow line. The cadre continually walked behind us and screamed for us to finish up and get out as we hurriedly gobbled down our food. This sucked—I wanted to get my hands on that recruiter. I didn't even have time to know whether the food was any good!

The first five days of basic training were especially miserable because of soreness from the shots and incision. We learned that the small sticks each cadre member carried were called "swagger sticks," which frequently left their impressions on our bodies during drill. Sergeant Hernandez proudly described his stick as a negative motivator. The sticks must have worked because in fewer than two weeks, the entire platoon was marching in perfect cadence.

Private Saul Johnson from New York City summoned the courage to ask Sergeant Hernandez if it was legal for them to strike us. Sergeant Hernandez grabbed Johnson by the collar and shoved him out the barracks door. We could hear Sergeant Hernandez screaming at the hapless fellow, ordering him to run to the orderly room. A few minutes later Johnson burst into the barracks and fell onto the floor gasping for breath and bleeding from his nose. Later, he informed us that according to the first sergeant, our drill instructors could do anything to us they deemed necessary to include pummeling our miserable bodies with swagger sticks. Nobody ever dared question Sergeant Hernandez again.

The remainder of basic training was a blur of getting up before dawn, performing calisthenics, running in formation, washing clothes, scrubbing our barracks, close-order drilling, attending classes on a wide range of subjects, running obstacle courses, going on long marches, learning how to shoot a variety of weapons, practicing hand-to-hand combat, wolfing down meals, and enjoying every precious minute of sleep.

Taking communal showers was a new experience for me. However, after a short time the novelty wore off and we began thinking of one another as fellow marines and less as members of the opposite sex. Still, Brenda Chan and Linda Sanchez were really good-looking women with athletic bodies. My day was complete if I was able to stand next to either one in the shower!

Everybody had to pull his or her own weight. At first only a few of the women and about half the men could do the requisite number of pushups. Gradually, their upper body strength improved and the number of repetitions they were able to perform increased. Although I am convinced our drill cadre was selected for their innate sadism, their ability to motivate was without equal. After a few weeks of training the entire platoon could run for miles without losing anyone. Only two people failed to keep up with the physical training. After four weeks they were discharged and sent home.

Sergeant Hernandez and corporals Turner and Ramos gave us little time to socialize but I made a few friends during basic training. It's impossible to spend twelve weeks with thirty-seven people and not make friends. Although we knew first and last names, during basic training we called one another by last name only. After basic, we were scattered throughout the Marine Corps.

I do remember one incident where our hand-to-hand combat instructor got the surprise of his life. One of the women in my platoon, Private Angel Sagura from Waco, Texas, knocked the instructor unconscious during a one-on-one exercise. I later heard that Sagura was assigned as a permanent member of the combat instruction faculty.

About halfway through basic training, we were herded into a classroom and given a battery of tests. Corporal Turner told us that we should do our best on each test because the outcome would help the "personnel pukes" decide what job we were best suited for.

After receiving permission to speak, Rafferty asked about the job he was promised by his recruiter. That was the first time I heard Corporal Turner laugh. Afterward she said, "While recruiters correctly informed you of the jobs in the marines, the service doesn't put idiots in jobs beyond their performance capability! And while I doubt any of you could handle anything more complicated than laundry or cleaning toilets, you should try your best on the tests. You never know; some of you maggots may get lucky."

After the tests were completed, we were told that the results would be made available at the end of basic training.

Back at the barracks, I asked Sanchez what job she wanted. She replied, "I don't know for sure, but I hope it has something to do with people and computers."

"That's an odd combination, don't you think?"

"No, communications would accommodate both desires. What about you, Hawkins?"

"I'm hoping for reconnaissance. I love the idea of sneaking around and gathering intelligence on the enemy."

"You want to be a spy?"

"Hey, it's not a dirty word or a bad job. In fact, most military victories have been achieved by one side having better intelligence than the other side."

"Relax. I was just pulling your chain!"

Graduation was a big event. A brass band played as we marched on the parade field and passed by the reviewing stand. Even Sergeant Hernandez appeared satisfied. He was probably glad to see us go.

After graduation, each marine reported to the now familiar white administrative building where we turned in our field gear and received our orders.

Getting orders was a novel experience. I entered an office and reported to a marine captain. It was Captain Whittaker! He said, "Private Hawkins, please be at ease." He continued. "I have good news for you. Based on your exceptional test score, you're being assigned to communications school in Texas. Congratulations on receiving an outstanding vocational assignment. You have been selected to attend a three-month course and embark on an enviable career in the marines as a communications specialist."

I was in shock. This was not the job I wanted! I almost blurted out that communications seemed like a sissy job, but this was an officer, and I didn't want to contradict him or piss him off.

Captain Whittaker noticed my expression and said, "So you are thinking that communications is not the job for a trained killer such as yourself?"

I replied, "*Sir, yes sir!*"

He smiled and said, "Private Hawkins, you have been trained to kill the enemy. Each year you will receive refresher training that will hone those skills. But the marines need people with multiple skills. By virtue of your intelligence, your attitude, and your demonstrated performance, you are qualified for one of the most challenging jobs in the marines. If it's any consolation, you will always be considered first and foremost an infantryman. But you should understand that we have to communicate if we are going to be an effective fighting force. Further, only a few are chosen to serve as communications specialists in the Space Marines."

I was shocked beyond numb. "Sir, did you say, Space Marines?"

Captain Whittaker grinned and slowly nodded.

I replied in a loud voice, "*Yes sir. Thank you, sir!*" Oh man, oh man—I was going to the Space Marines! Fewer than 1 percent of marines were selected for that elite unit.

Captain Whittaker got up and walked around his desk and placed the coveted Space Marines emblem on the Velcro patch located on my right chest. My thoughts were racing and it was difficult to focus. I did manage to shake his hand while grinning from ear to ear.

"Sir, how was I chosen for Space Marines?"

"It was a combination of two things. One was your test scores, but most importantly, it was the recommendation of Drill Sergeant Hernandez. We put a lot of faith in the recommendations of our instructional cadre. In this case, Sergeant Hernandez and I go way back and I trust his judgment implicitly."

I was dumfounded. I couldn't remember any special conversation

Sergeant Hernandez and I had during basic training. I continually worked to avoid bringing any attention to myself. *Oh well, thank you, Sergeant Hernandez!*

He then picked up a handheld device from the desk and recorded my basic training data—twelve weeks of accumulated pay, my travel orders, money for meals during travel, and an airline ticket—onto my imbedded chip.

He said, "Private Hawkins, your medical records were recorded during the implant and a duplicate of all this information will be stored in a central database at marine headquarters. Ticket agents use scanners for military travelers, so you will let the Phoenix Airport ticket agent scan your arm in order to board your flight to San Angelo, Texas. Civilians will also use scanners on your arm when you make purchases. The amount of purchase is deducted from your Marine Corps checking account. Needless to say, watch your purchases and don't try to spend more than you have because the marines hold deadbeats in low esteem."

I asked about the security of information stored in the chip.

He said, "Only selected data contained in the chip, such as your name, rank, checking account number, blood type, and transportation tickets are available to commercial scanners. All other data, such as your training history, assignments, performance appraisals, medical records, savings account, and test scores are encrypted. Those files are only accessible to scanners used by the UAR military. Good luck, Marine!"

I left the administrative building and loaded on a waiting bus being filled with my fellow platoon members. During the trip to Phoenix, we spent the time talking about our varied assignments and promising to stay in touch. Several of my buddies were envious of my new Space Marines patch and spent time kidding me about my having to bribe personnel to give me that assignment.

Linda Sanchez was also selected for the Space Marines and would attend communications school with me. While congratulating one another, I couldn't keep a big grin off my face. What a piece of luck!

Happiness was saying good-bye to Fort Sonora.

CHAPTER 2
A Corporate Demotion

Rolf Peters mentally squirmed under the glare of fifteen pairs of eyes sitting around the conference table. He felt beads of sweat run down his face and neck as he vainly tried to answer the question posed by Mr. Von Stubben.

"Mr. Peters, you're wasting my time. Your supervisor has assured me that you, as the lead project engineer, were given adequate resources to research the problem and find a solution. Today you're standing before this board and can't answer the simplest question. Once again, Mr. Peters, what is causing the carbon valves to stick? As you should know, we cannot afford to have any aspect of our mining operation fail. A single failure along the chain of critical events will cause the entire operation to fail. If the carbon valve sticks, the rocket fuel will not flow to the combustion chamber, and we cannot retrieve the asteroid for processing on the moon."

"Mr. Von Stubben, ladies and gentlemen, we have redesigned the faulty relay switch connected to the fuel intake valve. I am confident that the switch is almost 100 percent reliable. However, I have not heard anything about a fault in the carbon valve." There—he said it. He knew his boss would give him hell later but he was not going to stand in front of the CEO of Transvaal and take the blame for something that was not his fault.

Mr. Von Stubben slowly turned to Rolf's boss, Mr. Ainsley, who was sitting away from the conference table.

Without waiting for the inevitable question, Mr. Ainsley stood, cleared his throat, and said, "Mr. Von Stubben, ladies and gentlemen, Mr. Peters is a young man with an excellent academic background. I predict he will make us all proud someday. As his supervisor, I accept responsibility for his failure to fully investigate the problems with the rocket fuel system. Obviously I failed to provide the close supervision a person of his youth and inexperience needs. Although he was given verbal and written instructions to investigate the rocket fuel system, I failed to provide him adequate supervision." With that said, Mr. Ainsley sat down.

Mr. Von Stubben swung around to Mr. Peters and said, "Mr. Peters, your supervisor has given you a fine example to follow. Rather than blame someone else for his shortcomings, he accepted responsibility. Young man, this is something you have yet to learn.

"Rather than have this valuable lesson wasted, I am going to give you one chance to redeem yourself." After checking his calendar, he continued. "Starting next week, you will report for space training at our Sahara facility. We have a special three-month course designed for our lunar employees, and I am most anxious for you to attend this training course. Further, because you have wasted valuable time that has cost us considerable mining revenues, you will spend not one but two years at our lunar mining facility. This should give you more time to mature, reflect on what happened today, and gain valuable mining experience. Mr. Peters, have you any questions before you're dismissed?"

"No, Mr. Von Stubben. Everything is perfectly clear."

The stinging rebuke by the CEO and the public humiliation of being disciplined in front of the board of directors and his boss caused Rolf's ears and face to remain bright red throughout the elevator decent to the lobby. He barely remembered hearing his boss tell him to have a good weekend and to stay out of trouble. There was only one thing on Rolf's mind as he got in his car and raced away from corporate headquarters: *I'll make you old bastards pay for this someday,* he swore.

This two-year sentence on the moon was a clear signal that Rolf had been taken off the fast track to top management and that he may never regain his status with the corporation. That was the most depressing thought imaginable and one that put him into a killing rage.

CHAPTER 3
The Pickup

Rolf stopped at the first bar he saw after leaving the corporate headquarters. It was a Friday evening and he needed a drink.

The place was dark and most of the tables were already occupied. Rolf found a stool at the bar and ordered a double whiskey on the rocks.

The bartender quickly filled his order and placed a bowl of nuts near his drink. "Mister, do you want a check now or run a tab?"

Rolf glared at the bartender and said, "A tab and make me another drink."

Two years on the moon! Those smug old fools in the boardroom had wrecked all of his plans. Did he think Carol would wait two years for him? Hell no!

Carol Schmidt was the daughter of the Johannesburg city manager. She enjoyed a life of privilege and was accustomed to receiving the finest in service and material things. In a word, she was a beautiful but spoiled woman who would inevitably find someone else while he was exiled to the moon. In fact, Rolf doubted she would wait until he completed his training before a whole assortment of eligible young men started panting after her. He had a date with her on Saturday. That would be as good a time as any to break the bad news.

Rolf thought, *If I were less ambitious, I would just quit the corporation and find another job. I could work at a bank, farm, department store, or do almost any other job. They only problem is Transvaal Mining is the number one corporation in the entire country. Mining is king and all other businesses pale compared to the perks offered by mining.*

A few minutes later an attractive blonde sat on a stool next to him and asked for a light. Rolf took a book of matches from the bar and struck a match for her. Her hands felt good on his as she bent to light her cigarette. The warm smile she gave him afterward was another bonus.

She said, "Hi, my name is Deidre. And you are?"

"Rolf. Can I buy you a drink?"

Deidre was easy to talk to and time flew by as they got to know one another. They eventually left the bar and went to Rolf's apartment.

Lying on the bed, Rolf began thinking about the evening and his uncanny luck in meeting Deidre. His suspicions aroused, Rolf waited until Deidre went into the bathroom before rummaging through her purse.

Found it! The identification card proved that Transvaal employed Deidre and she worked in Department 5. Rolf knew that Department 5 dealt with corporate security. *Uh oh, this is not good,* he thought. Because of his anger at being demoted and sentenced to two years on the moon, he may have said too many things this evening that could spell big trouble if his words ever got back to the company.

Rolf quickly dressed and was waiting for Deidre when she returned from the bathroom.

Deidre's smile was quickly replaced by a startled look when she noticed the gun in Rolf's hand.

"Get dressed and be quick about it!"

"Rolf, what's happening?"

Rolf walked over to Deidre and slapped her hard across the face. "Bitch, I told you to get dressed! Do I need to say it again?"

Deidre began crying as she got dressed.

Rolf grabbed her purse and shoved her toward the door. He said, "If you know what's good for you, you'd better keep quiet and don't try running. I know how to use this gun."

Rolf stayed slightly behind Deidre as they walked to his car in the parking garage. Neither spoke until they reached his car.

Rolf opened the driver's door, threw Deidre's purse in the back, and held the gun pointed toward her as he carefully sat down. "Get in."

"Where are you taking me?"

Rolf didn't answer. He was too busy thinking of how to get this job finished. He started the motor and drove to a vacant manufacturing facility several miles from the city.

After parking the car, Rolf and Deidre entered a huge space through an open door. The concrete floor of the deserted factory had gaping holes where manufacturing equipment had been removed. It was littered with trash. They entered a dilapidated office in the rear of the building.

He pointed to an empty crate and said, "Sit down; we have to talk." He opened Deidre's purse, took out her identification card, and said, "I want to know everything."

A couple of hours later, Rolf was satisfied that he had extracted the truth from Deidre. From a bruised and swollen face, with a trickle of blood dripping from her chin, she had given him her entire mission.

Apparently, Mr. Ainsley had suspected that Rolf was getting in over his head and not concentrating on his job. As a precaution, he had asked his old friend, who ran security at Transvaal, to have someone check on Rolf after work. Deidre had been watching him for the past two weeks. Rolf thought, *Well, Ainsley, that's another one I owe you.*

Rolf's gun hand was slightly shaking when he looked once more at Deidre and said, "Baby, this just ain't your day." A single bullet fired from the small caliber gun sounded very loud in the office as Deidre slumped to the floor. However, Rolf doubted that the sound carried outside the old building.

He grabbed one of Deidre's arms and dragged her to a hole in the concrete floor. After dumping her in the hole, he took a can of gasoline from the trunk of his car and poured it over her lifeless body. He added some wooden crates and broken pieces of furniture to make sure the fire burned long enough to do its job.

The lit match ignited Deidre's remains, and the smell of burning flesh was overwhelming. Rolf stayed long enough to make sure the hot fire consumed the contents of Deidre's purse and her features.

Once back home Rolf thoroughly cleaned his apartment and car to eliminate every trace of Deidre's visit. Afterward he poured himself a drink and began thinking of a good story that would be plausible and easy to remember.

It took several hours before Rolf calmed down enough to begin thinking clearly. He knew he would be questioned on Monday; Tuesday at the latest.

Rolf reasoned, *The best story is to tell some truth but omit key details and lie about others. The story has to sound logical, flow, and remain consistent each time it's told. I must not memorize each word. The best story is slightly different each time it is told; not in the important details but leaving out an insignificant item this time or the next is natural and my story has to come across as truthful. My life depends on it.*

Rolf muttered to himself, "Well, Mr. Ainsley, you and Mr. Leher can sit around and wonder what happened to your precious Deidre while I'm wasting two years of my life on the moon. I don't believe you old farts have enough combined intellect to solve a crossword puzzle, much less solve a real murder. I suspect you got your corporate promotions by being subservient 'yes men' to your bosses. I have proven that I don't kowtow to anyone. You may have pushed me off track temporarily, but I will be back someday and I will have my revenge on everybody who screwed me. Deidre was unlucky enough to be the first on my list."

CHAPTER 4
Goodfellow Base

During the flight to San Angelo, I sat next to a rancher who loved to talk about his herd of cattle and problems with getting good help. The flight attendant served us drinks after takeoff. I ordered a beer, the first I'd had in months. The flight attendant scanned my arm and deducted the cost from my chip. That cold beer tasted great! Sanchez was sitting several rows behind me so I didn't get a chance to speak with her.

The rancher said, "What branch of the military are you in, sonny?"

I replied that I was a Space Marine.

He said, "Have you been to the moon?"

I grinned and said, "Not yet, sir. I've just completed basic training and am on my way to Goodfellow Base for communications training. I don't know where I'll be assigned after school."

He responded that the government was spending a lot of tax dollars on us and may not be getting its money's worth.

I jokingly replied, "If you knew how little I was getting paid, you might call your representative and demand our pay be raised."

He didn't like my smart-ass response and our conversation lapsed.

It was a smooth flight. The plane landed at San Angelo airport on time. Sanchez and I went to the luggage carousel and grabbed our duffel bags and walked to the ground transportation area. Several sailors were also there and we boarded a military van that was waiting at the curb.

Twenty minutes later we approached the base. From the outside, there was not much to see. Seemingly miles and miles of low grassland and scrub brush sprouting a high chain link fence topped by barbed wire. In the distance, some low buildings painted white were surrounded by a large collection of towers and wires. The road from the airport led to a concrete gatehouse with signs announcing the entrance to Goodfellow Base and warning people not to trespass. A gate guard ordered us out of the van and screened each chip for positive identification. We were informed that this was a secure base and nobody was allowed on or off without authorization.

The van took us to a large air-conditioned administrative building where we were given an in-processing briefing. "Welcome to Goodfellow Base. My name is Corporal James White. I am the detachment's administrative clerk. While you're here you will be assigned to the twenty-first student communications detachment commanded by Navy Lieutenant Raymond Sinclair. The first sergeant's name is Sergeant Lance Whitworth. They will exercise command and control over you outside the classroom. At this time, I am handing out maps of the base. This map shows all the pertinent places that will be discussed in this briefing."

He passed out the maps and we each took a copy.

"After receiving your security clearances, you will be enrolled in communications class. Prior to attending class, you will be assigned to various work details here on base. The duty roster is posted on the bulletin board located outside the orderly room. Read it first thing every morning and each evening before turning in.

"I need to warn you about missing work details. If you miss a work assignment, you will be given additional work details and will be restricted to base for the duration of your training. If you miss a second work assignment, you will be sent back to basic training for a four-week refresher course."

That got my attention! Quickly glancing around, I noticed the others were now paying attention too.

"During your first six weeks, you will not be allowed to leave the base for any reason. We maintain good relations with the locals and don't want a bunch of crazed men and women disrupting their lives.

We know from experience that it takes a while for pent-up emotions created by basic training to dissipate. The last thing Lieutenant Sinclair wants to do is meet the father of some pregnant girl whose misfortune began with dating one of you Romeos!"

Everybody burst out laughing at that comment. I began to think that maybe this place wasn't going to be so bad.

"At the end of each month, your pay will be wirelessly entered on your chip via the UAR military pay system. At any time you can decide how much of your pay you want to put into your cash account. If you want to make an allotment or enroll in a savings plan, see the First Sergeant.

"Hours for the mess hall are breakfast from 0530 to 0700, lunch from 1130 to 1300, and dinner from 1800 to 1930 seven days a week. We have a reputation at Goodfellow Base for having the 'best chow in the West.'

"Here on base you are authorized to use the laundry, base theater, chapel, enlisted club, barber shop, and base exchange. They're highlighted on your maps. I advise you not to purchase large objects. Previous students have donated a lot of stuff to local charities because they couldn't carry it with them to their next assignment. You will need to purchase razors, soap, and other toiletries. While these were furnished to you in basic, you are now responsible for buying them.

"The supply room is located next to the orderly room. After this briefing, you need to stop by and get your issue of sheets, blankets, pillow, pillowcase, and towels." He explained laundry procedures and how to replace worn clothing. Then he said, "A field jacket and gloves will be issued to you on the first of October. That's the date it officially becomes cold."

We all laughed at his dry humor. You could tell this guy had made the same speech numerous times. He had his lines down pat.

He then gave us our room assignments and I learned I would be bunking in Barracks 6 with Seaman Carla Wells. he warned us to be considerate of our barracks-mates and to keep noise levels to a minimum. "Fraternizing" was also highly discouraged and could result in our repeating basic training.

"First Sergeant Whitworth makes daily inspections of the barracks. A word to the wise: don't get on his bad side! A sheet of paper is attached to the door of your closets. Ensure that you arrange your gear accordingly. And keep your rooms clean! A clean-up roster for hallways, front entrance, and latrine will be posted on the door to the latrine—or 'head' to you marines and sailors. Any questions?"

After the briefing, I introduced myself to Seaman Carla Wells. I said, "Hi. It looks like we're going to be roommates."

She grinned and said, "Hello, Jim. Glad to meet you. Just call me CW. Where are you from?"

"Mississippi."

Thus started the "getting to know you" conversation known and practiced throughout the world.

CW and I got our duffel bags and walked to the supply room with the others and picked up our linens. This was a different experience from basic in that the stuff was handed to us and not thrown in our faces. After having our chips scanned, we walked to our room and checked it out.

The barracks was air-conditioned! Our room had two single beds with eight-inch mattresses, two closets, and two small desks with chairs and lamps. The floor was a highly polished tile and the room was very clean. I felt like I had checked into a luxury hotel!

"Jim, would you look at this?" CW asked. "I spent my last six weeks of basic training aboard an old navy ship and we were packed together like sardines! I never expected this."

We dropped our linens and duffel bags and checked out the head. It too was spotless. There was a long row of sinks, a communal shower, and individual toilet stalls. We checked the duty roster on the door and our names had already been added near the bottom of the list. Cleanup detail was assigned in pairs. Each week the latrine detail would rotate to the next pair of roommates.

Our next stop was to visit the post exchange for toiletries and other stuff. I picked up soap, disposable razors, a comb, toothbrush, toothpaste, deodorant, military-style watch and a small radio. CW bought the same things and added hygiene napkins and an assortment of e-post cards. The e-post cards were pre-paid pictures of Goodfellow Base and San Angelo. You simply write your message and forwarding address on them and then feed them through any scanner. After having our chips scanned for the cost of our purchases, we went back to our room and got it squared away.

By this time it was 1730 and CW asked if I wanted to check out the enlisted club. I said sure and we headed over.

Things were pretty noisy inside. A country and western song was playing on the jukebox and loud conversations came from several groups. One group in particular seemed to be having a good time. They were sitting at a large table. I recognized them as the other new arrivals. One of them noticed us and invited us to their table. They were sharing a pitcher of beer. We were offered mugs and I bought the next round. We introduced ourselves to Donahue, Everette, Finnes, and Sanchez. It was fun sitting there and sharing our memories of basic training. I noticed that the sailors had a similar basic training experience to us marines, but they had a different location for their training. Sanchez and I found ourselves slightly exaggerating the misery endured by us marines, and I'm sure the sailors did too. One thing was clear: Goodfellow Base was a lot different from Fort Sonora! At Fort Sonora, we were never allowed unsupervised free time or the opportunity to drink beer. At Goodfellow, we were treated like adults.

At 1900, we decided to go to the mess hall. Another pleasant surprise! We had a selection of food and it was great! I noticed that the people on kitchen police (KP) stayed busy clearing tables and filling containers. We decided this detail didn't look so bad, especially in light of what we had experienced during basic training.

After dinner, CW, Sanchez, and Everette decided to take a walk, and Donahue, Finnes, and I went back to the barracks. Donahue and Finnes started quizzing me about my sleeping arrangements with CW, but I shrugged them off and changed the subject. We checked the bulletin board on the way to the barracks. Our names were posted. Donahue, Sanchez, and I had KP (starting at 0400) and CW, Everette, and Finnes were to report to the orderly room at 0700 for base clean-up detail. We went to the orderly room and arranged for a wake-up call at 0315.

Our details soon became a routine. Sometimes CW and I would be assigned together, but that was the exception. I began to understand how much work went into operating and maintaining this base. There was one detail in which all of us were involved. That was cleaning the barracks after a class had graduated. This was the only time we were permitted into another barracks. First Sergeant Whitworth demanded that the empty barracks and its rooms be spotless. It was an all-day job before he was satisfied.

One evening CW and I were alone in our room. We had been discussing possible future assignments when an awkward silence occurred.

Out of the blue, she said, "Jim, I want you to know I like you, and I've been wondering how you feel about me. You seem to enjoy my company but you haven't even made a pass at me!"

"I like you a lot. You're lots of fun to be around, and I've sometimes wondered what it would be like if we had a closer relationship." After pausing, I blurted, "I haven't said anything because I didn't want to pressure you into making a commitment or make a fool of myself in case you weren't interested."

CW smiled and said, "I'm glad we're having this conversation. I was beginning to think you weren't interested in girls! It's really great finding out you're only shy."

My face turned an even deeper shade of red and I tried to think of a snappy comeback.

CW laughed and walked over to the light switch, turned it off, and said, "I think it's time we got to know one another better, don't you?"

I can't remember answering her, but I was grateful that she wasn't shy like me.

CHAPTER 5
Saying Good-Bye

The flight to the Sahara training facility was long and boring. Rolf had time to think about his final days in Johannesburg.

As expected, Carol was not thrilled with the prospect of Rolf being gone for two years. "Rolf, will you get to come home on leave?"

"Unfortunately, the company doesn't permit anyone to take leave from the Transvaal Lunar Base. It's too expensive to make the trip. Minerals, equipment, and supplies have total priority." Rolf could see the disappointment on Carol's face, and he knew it was over between them. Carol was a spoiled, self-centered little bitch who would never dream of waiting for anyone! Whoever married her was in for a lifetime of servitude. They parted that evening with Carol tearfully promising to write often. Rolf was thinking, *Yeah, yeah. I'll believe that when it happens.*

Rolf was called into Mr. Ainsley's office on Monday morning, where he met Mr. Dieter Leher, the head of corporate security. Both Mr. Ainsley and Mr. Leher questioned him for more than an hour. It was a good thing he had mentally rehearsed his story. When the conversation got around to Deidre, Rolf readily admitted he'd met her at the singles bar on Friday and they'd had a few drinks. Rolf said they'd left the bar at the same time but lied when he told them he never saw her again. There was no way he was going to admit to taking Deidre to his apartment—and apparently, there was nobody who could say otherwise.

After the interrogation, Rolf was directed to a cubicle near his former office to complete some paperwork on the project and begin out-processing for his next assignment. He knew that Transvaal Security and the local police would conduct a thorough search for Deidre. He hoped they would never find the body.

After being called in to his former office, Rolf met his replacement, Sylvia Van Buren, the new fuel system project engineer. Sylvia was a mousy-haired, homely looking mechanical engineer with no personality. After answering some technical questions, Sylvia dismissed Rolf by extending her hand for a good-bye handshake.

As Rolf walked out of his former office, he had a nightmarish thought that this frumpy bitch would probably get all the credit for his work and be praised for "her" accomplishment. How revolting! He thought, *Oh well ... she's just another name for my list.*

By Tuesday, Rolf had completed out-processing. He arranged to have his personal belongings placed in long-term storage and canceled the lease on his apartment. No sense in paying money for an apartment he wouldn't need for two years. He spent his last night alone in a hotel near the airport.

CHAPTER 6
Training at al-Sidi

The flight finally arrived at Ghat Airport in the former Libya. As Rolf stepped out of the plane and stood on the tarmac, the hot air hit him like a giant fist. It was so hot and dry that the simple act of drawing a breath was almost painful. He had never felt heat like this. It was as though he'd died and gone to hell. The thermometer outside the building registered 113 degrees.

Inside the stifling terminal, Rolf made his way past men and women hurrying to catch their plane and clusters of families saying good-bye to loved ones. This airport was different from any others he had visited. A mixture of pungent odors ranging from sweaty bodies to native spices permeated the building. At places the scent was overpowering. Rolf was glad to get his bag from the carousel and proceed to the exit.

A scruffy man dressed in a Transvaal security uniform met him at the exit. Rolf produced his identification and was escorted to a bus and driven to the space training facility located about thirty miles from the airport. The air conditioner on the bus had seen better days—so had the bus. Mercifully, the road was paved and the trip took less than one hour.

Talk about being nowhere! The training camp was surrounded by a rusted fence. Inside the fence, all you could see was a few rows of tents, some portable toilets, and a large, nondescript, one-story concrete building located in the center of the compound.

Rolf knew the moon could not be more desolate than this North African sand pile! Looking around, he couldn't see any vegetation.

Von Stubben was a dead man! As Rolf walked to the concrete building, he couldn't decide if he should go through the door or turn around and head back to the airport. Either way, Von Stubben was going to die for putting him in this predicament.

"You there, what do you think this is, a vacation spa? Move your arse!"

Rolf looked up to see a sweat-stained, bearded man yelling at him to move faster.

The Sahara training facility was named al-Sidi. Why that name had been chosen nobody seemed to know or care. Later, Rolf overheard his fellow trainees corrupting the name to "all-sand."

Rolf was housed in a tent along with five other trainees. Mosquito netting was carefully arranged to keep out flies, scorpions, and snakes. The tent had a wooden floor that had to be swept daily in order to temporarily rid themselves of the ever-encroaching sand.

When Rolf entered his tent, it felt like a sauna. He spotted six wood-framed canvas cots arranged three to a side. Each cot had a name card attached to it facing the aisle. A small wooden footlocker was placed at the end of each cot. Rolf stopped at his cot and was looking at his name card when an Arab orderly entered his tent and silently handed Rolf a cloth bag. The orderly immediately turned around and left without saying a word.

Rolf dumped the contents of the bag on his cot and took a quick inventory. He found a broad-billed cap with a folding cloth neck protector, two loose-fitting shirts, two pair of trousers, a web belt, swim suit, sheath knife, sandals, razor, blades, soap, toothbrush, toothpaste, sunscreen, water purification tablets, compass, and a canteen. The cloth bag was to be used as a laundry bag.

A few minutes later Rolf's roommates began entering the tent. It was evident they had been at the facility for at least a day because they were already wearing clothing similar to what Rolf had been issued.

A non-commissioned officer entered the tent, and everybody jumped to attention. "Ah, I see we have our replacement! My name is Sergeant Hussein. I'll be your trainer during the next twelve weeks. What's your name?"

"My name is Rolf Peters and I—" Rolf couldn't finish the remainder of his sentence because his cheek was on fire after having been slapped by Sergeant Hussein's short leather riding whip. His hurt was quickly replaced by rage. Rolf stepped toward Sergeant Hussein and threw a punch at the grinning Arab's face. His punch missed and once again the whip did its work; this time on the side of Rolf's neck. Rolf fell to his knees in agony, tears running down his cheeks, his ears ringing.

He could barely hear Sergeant Hussein saying, "Mr. Peters, you will quickly change into your uniform and report to the dining hall with your fellow squad members. From this day forward, you will do exactly as you are told. And one more thing—you will show me a great deal of respect. Do you understand me, you fatherless son of a diseased whore?"

Rolf managed a weak, "Yes, sir."

"Excellent. I'm certain your teammates will give you a full briefing and will show you how to best survive in your new world."

As Rolf quickly changed into his uniform, the others told him about the routine and what was going on. They informed him that Sergeant Hussein had once been a major in the Libyan army and his family was among the ruling class of his country before it had been absorbed by Transvaal. Sergeant Hussein's comfortable world and privileged lifestyle evaporated when Transvaal became the major shareholder in Libya. After his savings disappeared, he was forced take this job offered by Transvaal in order to survive.

As they walked to the dining facility, Rolf asked numerous questions. His squad members seemed eager to talk and gave him some disturbing news about one of their missing members. It seems that Sergeant Hussein had taken the squad on a night march a few nights ago. The missing squad member was an attractive woman named Kitty who had a great smile and was friendly to everyone. Sergeant Hussein and Kitty had walked away from the others that evening, supposedly to scout some difficult terrain. About an hour later, Sergeant Hussein returned to the other squad members and informed them that Kitty had been bitten by a viper and had died. Back at camp, there was no mention of her disappearance. An orderly collected her things, and it was as if she had never existed. Rolf immediately began thinking about how he might use this information as leverage against Sergeant Hussein.

Rolf's squad consisted of four men and a woman. Of the men, Hussein and Ibrahim were Arabs; Pieter was a Boer; and Solly was an African. The woman was a tall, muscular African and not attractive. Her name was Shanna, and she had disfiguring tribal scars carved into her face. However, her disfigurement didn't seem to bother the men. They actually competed with one another for her favors. After spending his first night with the squad members, it became clear to Rolf that Shanna called the shots—the man who'd pleased her most that day was invited to her cot that evening.

Rolf's squad members were being trained for assignments as miners or technicians, with duty at the company's lunar base. Rolf was the only member of the squad in Transvaal management. He kept that fact from the others because he couldn't afford to have them believe he felt superior to them. That would be an open invitation to avoid helping him at a most critical point during the training. When asked, Rolf lied and said he was a metals-processing technician.

A loudspeaker attached to the side of the building played weird trumpet notes obviously designed to wake the dead. The six squad members climbed out from under their mosquito nets and hurriedly dressed. Putting on trousers, shirt, and sandals and grabbing a hat on the way out was done in fewer than two minutes. The six squad members lined up in front of their tent and awaited Sergeant Hussein's appearance.

After Sergeant Hussein described the day's events, the squad was permitted to visit the portable toilets before walking to the dining facility. A water basin with soap and towels was a mandatory stop before getting food. Heaven help the poor bastard who forgot to wash his or her hands before eating. Sergeant Hussein took a great deal of pleasure in monitoring and providing on-the-spot corrections designed to improve his squad's hygiene habits. Rolf had him pegged as a sadist who reveled in bullying people.

Breakfast consisted of overripe figs, tasteless yogurt, small hard rolls, and strong coffee. The food was edible but the same menu every morning quickly became monotonous.

Mercifully, a majority of the training facility was underground. The elevator ran from the ground floor down two levels. The kitchen, storage, and a heavily guarded elevator shaft entrance were on the ground floor. Below ground, administrative offices and classrooms were on the first level. On the second level, Rolf discovered a fully equipped gym and an Olympic-sized swimming pool.

After breakfast, the squad was taken down to the second level for a class on spacesuit maintenance. Afterward they were assigned to various pieces of gym equipment and exercised according to pre-established plans. Each person had undergone a physical screening, and a plan had been created to meet his or her individual needs. Sergeant Hussein walked among his squad to ensure all exercises were completed according to the plan.

Being in top physical condition, Rolf enjoyed the hand-to-hand combat. He had studied karate in Johannesburg and was able to beat each member of his squad. Only the instructor was able to win sparring matches against Rolf.

Learning how to fight with a knife was a unique experience. Squad members were expected to become proficient with knives and guns. Each person took his and her turn with a specialist in edged weapons. Hard rubber knives were used. The instructors were experts, and when they stabbed you with the practice knife, it hurt! To avoid pain from being stabbed, trainees worked hard to improve their abilities. After three weeks of daily practice, they were given real knives and introduced to men who also had real knives.

Sergeant Hussein addressed the squad. "The men you face today are convicted criminals who have been condemned to death for their crimes. They have been told that the only way they will ever see another day and win a pardon is to win inside this ring. I'm telling you the same thing. Only one person comes out of the ring alive. Rolf, you piece of camel dung, you're first."

Rolf wasted no time in dispatching his opponent. When it comes down to it, the more skilled and determined man wins a knife fight. Rolf demonstrated his survival instincts for the others to witness. The fact that he showed no emotion over killing another human being was not lost on the squad members or Sergeant Hussein.

One after another, each squad member proved his or her worth. Shanna's opponent was a huge Arab with an obvious limp. However, after a few parries, it was clear that he knew how to use a knife. The fight ended when her opponent made a mistake and missed her with a lunge. Shanna stepped inside his outstretched arm and stabbed him under his ribcage. Game over. Rolf led the others in cheering for her victory.

Solly's opponent was a big, white South African. Solly's good nature exhibited itself in the ring. His opponent slipped under his guard and cut him deeply with a wide slicing motion. Leaping backward in pain, Solly crouched, ready for the next attack. As his opponent came in to finish him, Solly suddenly stepped forward, blocked his opponent's arm, and gave him a wicked thrust under his chin. Solly was taken to the infirmary and sewn up. His wound limited his physical activity for two weeks.

After that gruesome adventure, each day was similar to the one before. Classes on equipment operation and maintenance, physical fitness, and combat training were everyday occurrences. The biggest event each week was a map-reading exercise.

Map reading at night in the desert is scary. A bus would take the squad out of the compound. Its windows were painted over so they had no idea of the direction or distance the bus traveled from the compound. Once the bus stopped, the squad was given a map and instructions to get back to the compound, although traveling at night was infinitely preferable to walking in the heat of the day. With no landmarks to guide them, the squad was forced to rely upon their compass, location of stars, and any hints given by the instructor. With only one canteen of water for each person, getting back to the compound was of paramount importance.

After ten weeks of nonstop physical activity, the squad members were lean, in excellent physical shape, and dangerous. The remaining two weeks were spent in the pool gaining familiarity with using their space suits. Each squad member was given a task to complete underwater. To make the activity more exciting, the instructor had a remote switch that controlled the oxygen valve on each space suit. Knowing that someone could cut off your oxygen supply if you were not performing at your best was a strong motivator.

Rolf's knowledge of mechanics, personal combat, and his leadership skills were recognized by his squad members, and he was informally chosen to be their leader. Nobody ever said anything; they just came to acknowledge him as their leader. His position was evident outside the pool too. One of the perks was being summoned to Shanna's cot more often than the other men. While Shanna's disfigured face was a definite turn-off, her muscular body was pure pleasure.

CHAPTER 7
Recruitment

After four weeks of seemingly endless work details interspersed with wonderful evenings with CW, I received a message to report to the orderly room.

Corporal White introduced me to Major Richard Simpson, who took me into a small office and closed the door.

Major Simpson asked me to sit down. He said, "Private Hawkins, what I'm about to tell you is highly classified. You're not to discuss this with anyone. Is that clear?"

"Yes, sir."

"Your security clearance has been finalized, and you will attend the next communications class. However, there is something else I want to discuss with you."

Expectantly, I answered, "Sir?"

"Jim, when you joined the marines, you stated that you were interested in reconnaissance. Are you still interested in that field?"

"Yes, sir. I am."

"I work for intelligence division, which is staffed by a small group of men and women. We work directly for the commander of the Space Marines, and our existence is known to very few people. Our primary job is collecting and analyzing intelligence data.

"Here is a typical scenario in which intelligence division is involved. As you may know, Jupiter Corporation has a government contract to deliver personnel and mining equipment to the moon.

Also, they're responsible for locating and transporting ore-rich asteroids from the asteroid belt to the moon. Ray Corporation, or RAYCO, has a government contract to operate and maintain ore-processing equipment. Lastly, Jupiter is under contract to bring processed materials back to Earth. During the past six months, the news media has reported some problems with corporate employees on the moon."

"Yes, sir, I remember seeing something in the news about a problem up there."

Major Simpson nodded and continued. "We suspect that some employees within RAYCO are secretly discussing a deal with one of the mega-corporations. This deal, if it occurs, has the potential of putting our moon base and our nation's mining operations either out of business or under the control of a mega-corporation. We can't allow that to happen."

"So tell me—what would you do to prevent a hostile takeover of our mining operations?"

"Sir, I believe you need to find out who the traitor is and then take him out. I appreciate your asking me for a solution, but I don't understand why. I'm just a private in the Space Marines."

"I know who and what you are. Your potential value to us is why we're having this conversation. You may not have realized it, but you're being interviewed for membership. I want to know if you are interested in and capable of becoming an operative working for Space Marines' intelligence division."

"Sir, what would I do as an operative?"

"The abbreviated version is, your primary job would be to gather intelligence, report findings, and take any action as directed by intelligence division."

"This sounds a lot like reconnaissance."

"Correct. As an operative, your job would include reconnaissance. But it would also include gathering intelligence from a variety of sources; not just visual observations."

"Sir, I also understand reporting findings. What about 'taking any action as directed'?"

"Sometimes our field agents must act in order to prevent a catastrophe. We don't always have the luxury of 'calling in the marines,' so to speak. Sometimes we're required to personally complete the job."

"Sir, I'm very interested in joining intelligence division."

"I'm glad you want to join our team. I can promise you an interesting career."

Finally it seemed that I was heading for a big adventure and not consigned to a career of being a mere communications specialist! "Sir, what do I have to do?"

Major Simpson smiled, as he said, "Nothing, Jim, absolutely nothing." Then, after pausing for a few moments, he said, "Well, that's not entirely accurate.

"Everything at our end has been taken care of. In order to put your cover story in place, the first thing you have to do is miss KP tomorrow." Major Simpson handed me a small envelope. "I want you to take the sleeping pill inside this envelope before you turn in tonight. This will guarantee that you miss KP in the morning. And don't let anyone see you take the pill. From now on, you'll be asked to do many things that, at first, won't make a whole lot of sense."

I numbly accepted the envelope and put it in my pocket.

"You'll be put on report and kept here on base for the next three months. And because you won't be going off base and will be given extra duty, nobody will suspect that you will be attending intelligence classes in addition to the normal communications training."

Stunned, I didn't say anything for a while. CW and I had been planning to celebrate our first liberty this weekend. We even had reservations at the best restaurant in San Angelo!

Major Simpson must have sensed my dilemma. His face softened as he said, "Jim, I know it's tough. I also went through this training and know how important it is to get off base and see civilians. If there was a better way to get this job done, we wouldn't be having this conversation."

"Sir, what about my friends? They'll think I'm some kind of dirtbag for missing formation!"

"I'm sorry. Only you and I will know the truth. Your friends do not have clearance for this."

"Sir, why can't my friends know? They have security clearances too."

"You've been selected and cleared for this top-secret assignment.

In the intelligence division, we don't tell anyone anything unless they need to know. This includes your special friend, CW. Besides, how do you know one or more of your friends isn't a corporate sympathizer? And even if they aren't, what about their friends or their families? No, the best way is to keep this strictly between you and me."

Major Simpson slid a piece of paper over to me and asked me to sign just above my name.

I looked at the paper and noticed that it was an official-looking form swearing me to secrecy and threatening all sorts of punishment if I failed to keep my promise.

"Jim, by signing this paper, you're volunteering for service in the intelligence division of the Space Marines and are promising to never reveal to the public anything about your work."

I was in a state of shock as I read and then signed the form. I returned to my barracks. Of course I wanted the excitement of serving as an intelligence operative, but I was depressed about what I had been told to do.

While walking back, I asked myself, *How did Major Simpson know about CW?*

CHAPTER 8
Missing KP

I can't begin to describe how difficult it was to deliberately miss reporting for KP at 0400 the next morning.

I waited until nobody was around before swallowing the pill and flushing the envelope. I then returned to my room and promptly fell asleep.

CW shook me awake me at 0600 and said, "Jim, aren't you supposed to be on KP this morning?"

I looked at my watch and said, "Oh shit! Oh shit!"

She said I'd better move it and hope the mess sergeant is a forgiving soul.

As I scrambled out of my bed and began dressing, our door opened and Corporal White entered. "Private Hawkins, you are late for detail. Report to the first sergeant in the orderly room *and I mean right now, mister!*"

As I dashed through the orderly room door, I saw First Sergeant Whitworth sitting behind his desk. Standing at attention in front of his desk was Private Linda Sanchez. She didn't look at me as I stood beside her and also snapped to attention.

First Sergeant Whitworth looked as if he had lost his best friend. "I don't understand why you two failed to report for duty this morning. Your names were posted on the detail roster. You were told to check the roster before turning in each evening. What's your excuse? Did you think that just because you're starting class next week you didn't have to report for detail?"

There was a long pause. Sanchez didn't say anything. I said, "No excuse, First Sergeant. I failed to check the duty roster last night."

After a long pause, First Sergeant Whitworth said, "Well, that's just too bad. I'm really disappointed in both of you. As promised, you are both restricted for the duration of your tour here at Goodfellow Base. After your class begins, you will report to the school commandant for additional work detail.

"As for today, report to the mess hall for the remainder of your KP assignment. And ensure you check the roster before turning in tonight. Any questions? If not, you're dismissed."

Sanchez and I ran to the mess hall. The mess sergeant was waiting for us as we arrived. "Well, I'm glad you two sleepyheads finally decided to grace us with your presence. Sanchez, you're on pots and pans. Hawkins, congratulations—you get to clean the grease pit today."

KP duties are based on "first come, first served." The best duty is dining room orderly. In this job you keep the milk and orange juice dispensers filled and clean up spills. People on KP try to get to the mess hall first so they can get this cushy job. Pots and pans is the least desirable duty in the kitchen. These large, heavy containers require considerable elbow grease to clean them to the mess sergeant's satisfaction.

Cleaning the grease pit is easily the most hated job of all. It consists of opening metal grates that cover a portion of the drain line from the mess hall and scooping rancid grease into trash containers for disposal. It is a messy, all-day job. At the end of the day, your uniform and body stink to high heaven.

As I dragged into the room that night, CW was waiting for me. "Jim, I just can't understand why you overslept this morning. You always seem so conscientious about everything. Why did you oversleep?"

"Look, CW, I screwed up, okay? It won't happen again."

"It may not happen again, but you've really messed things up for us. Our plans for celebrating in San Angelo this weekend have been wrecked. Not having you with me during our first time off this base is a bunch of crap. Oh, and I heard that cute little Linda Sanchez also failed to report for KP this morning. What's going on, Jim? Am I missing something?"

Noticing how CW's eyes were blazing, I could tell that this was going to be even harder than the session with First Sergeant Whitworth. Oh crap. I knew that after CW finished her rant, I would be sleeping alone tonight.

After the bus left base on Saturday morning, I knocked on Sanchez's door and asked, "Do you want to go have breakfast?" She opened the door and grabbed her cap on the way out. We didn't speak until we were sitting down.

Sanchez said, "Jim, I feel horrible. Since joining the marines, I have never been late for any formation. And being confined to base for the remainder of our training really sucks!"

"I totally agree. They say, 'Let the punishment fit the crime,' but being confined for twelve weeks does seem a little harsh."

Linda smiled and said, "Well, I suspect you're paying a higher price than I am."

I thought, *You got that right!*

CHAPTER 9
Communications School

The following Monday morning we reported to class at 0730. A chain-link fence topped with spiraling rows of barbed tape surrounded the building. Everyone was excited as we entered through a gate adjacent to the guardhouse and had our chips scanned by an armed guard.

A sergeant met us at the front door of the building and directed us to a classroom. Inside, we sixteen students were introduced to the communications faculty.

"Ladies and gentlemen, welcome to communications school. My name is Captain Robert Stevens. I am the school commandant. This morning we're going to give you an orientation, which will be followed by reviewing your course syllabus.

"For the next three months, you will be trained in the latest communication theory, procedures, and equipment. Your classes will begin promptly at 0730 each day, Monday through Friday. You will be given one hour for lunch and your classes will end at 1600. You will be issued computers containing lesson materials that can be taken to your barracks for research and study. There will be weekly exams consisting of writing responses to questions and 'hands-on' practical exercises with actual equipment.

"At the end of your course, you will be assigned to a communications posting at a military site. Which site you are assigned will depend upon the needs of the air force, army, navy, or marines.

"At this time, I want to introduce our faculty."

"Dr. Wayne McKinnon will teach communication theory; Sergeant John Newsome will teach equipment operations; Mr. Vince Tanner will teach equipment maintenance; and Lieutenant Sandra Scott will teach communications operations. These instructors are communication experts with years of field experience and we are very fortunate to have them on the faculty. You will be divided into groups of four and will rotate among these instructors. Sergeant Emile Braun is my adjutant who handles administrative responsibilities.

"Open your syllabus, and let's go over your schedule. Privates Hawkins and Sanchez, report to my office at 1605 today."

I felt my face redden as my name was called out by the commandant. I'm sure Sanchez was also blushing but I didn't turn around to see her—I kept my eyes to the front of the classroom.

The remainder of the morning consisted of reviewing the class schedule, watching a film on communications history, and taking a tour of the communications labs where an amazing collection of equipment was crammed into each room. During the first day, we were issued our computers, which were small and rugged. The computer consisted of a one half-by-two inch wafer about one inch thick. It was designed to be inserted in our arm with metallic ink antenna and contact information tattooed on our skin. We were sent in pairs to the dispensary where a team of specialists surgically inserted the computers and tattooed the contact and antenna on our forearms. The contact accepted ancillary devices to include a special viewer. The antenna enabled us to operate in a wireless mode.

At 1605 Linda and I reported to Captain Stevens. He invited us into his office and closed the door. He said, "Okay, you two, please have a seat." As we sat, he smiled and congratulated us on being selected for intelligence training. "I know it's tough having to stay on base while your buddies go out and have fun. However, the Space Marines Intelligence Division has selected you for this special training, and we don't have much time to prepare you as communications intelligence specialists."

Linda and I looked at one another and began grinning. We had managed to keep our recruitment from one another! My respect for her increased.

Captain Stevens continued. "Your dinners will be delivered here and you will spend three additional hours each evening and six hours on Saturday and Sunday. Your extra classes will be demanding. Sergeant Braun will be your primary instructor. Please do not acknowledge him as an instructor outside his class. As far as the other students are concerned, he is my adjutant who types memos, reviews lesson plans for the faculty, orders supplies, et cetera. Incidentally, you should know that Sergeant Braun is a highly decorated marine with years of experience in communication intelligence."

I couldn't help but note the "secrets within secrets." This intelligence business would take some getting used to. "Starting tomorrow, your evening classes will begin. As of this evening, the first sergeant will move you two into the same room in the barracks. He is making the announcement so all you have to do is move your things."

Linda asked, "Sir, why do we have to move?"

Captain Stevens said, "Good question, Sanchez. I want you and Hawkins to move in together because we need to minimize questions that are bound to come from your classmates. Sharing the same room will reduce personal contact with others in the barracks. I hesitate to use the term 'isolation,' but that's what we're encouraging to some degree. Also, if one of you should talk in his or her sleep, there is less chance of something being overheard by an outsider.

"Again, please accept my sincere congratulations on your selection to the most elite intelligence outfit in the world."

Linda and I slowly walked back to the barracks after our meeting with Captain Stevens. We didn't talk much. We were both depressed and there was little to say.

At the barracks, Corporal White had already instructed Seaman Everette to move into my room, and he told me to move my things into room 108 with Private Sanchez.

It took maybe ten minutes for me to clear out and move in with Sanchez. CW didn't speak. The others had probably labeled Sanchez and me as losers.

After Corporal White left, CW and Everette came into our room and asked us if we were okay. I said, "Sure." Linda just nodded and only gave halfhearted responses to their attempts at conversation. After they left, Sanchez crawled into her bed and started crying. After studying for a half hour, I turned out the lights and went to bed thinking of CW.

Our next day started at 0530. After cleaning up and eating breakfast, we made it to class by 0725. Dr. McKinnon gave our first class. He was fascinating to listen to and you could immediately tell he had a vast store of knowledge.

At 1130 we walked to the mess hall, had lunch, and returned at 1220 for equipment instruction given by Sergeant Newsome.

This was the "fun" class. I have always enjoyed operating equipment. Sergeant Newsome was an artist with communication equipment. Our equipment classroom was set up into five complete workstations arranged along three walls. The instructor's workstation was easily visible by the students. Sergeant Newsome would demonstrate a few steps and would then walk around the room to make sure everybody was performing the same steps and not falling behind or getting ahead of the instruction. "By the numbers, people!" I've also heard this teaching technique referred to as "monkey see, monkey do."

Our communication equipment was completely dependent upon embedded computer systems. Although I'd used computers in high school, I'd never seen such sophisticated stuff. We had classes on a wide range of equipment to include miniature communications gear used by marine squads, base station equipment, landlines, microwave antennas, LANs, power systems, and the large transmitters/receivers used to communicate between Earth and the moon.

Pretty soon my head was crammed with terms such as multiplex, demodulator, double and single sideband, frequency hopping, phasing, parabolic, burst transmissions, wavelength, radio frequency interference (RFI), signal strength, wave propagation, satellite dish alignment, ionosphere, bouncing, lasers, line-of-sight, frequency drift, and many others.

One week after our computers were inserted into our arms, a specialist activated the computer, which became solely dedicated to its host. It's powered by the electrolytes in our bodies, enabling it to remain active on a constant basis. We spent a lot of time getting familiar with the computer, its embedded software, and various components.

Our personal computers became an integral part of our classes. In addition to course materials, they were loaded with maintenance programs that would help find equipment faults. This capability greatly simplified repair actions and enabled us to quickly restore communication systems to fully operational status (provided you had the replacement part on hand).

Every other day we had classes on communication operation and equipment maintenance. Communication operation is the administrative side of our new profession. Knowing frequency allocations, call signs, security classification levels, message formatting, transmission, and message handling were some topics we studied. Lieutenant Scott knew her stuff.

I didn't understand why a naval officer would need to know the administrative details and finally summoned the nerve to ask her. She stood and answered my question for the benefit of the whole class. "Ladies and gentlemen, Private Hawkins wants to know why a naval officer needs to know the administrative details of communication operations. I'm sure some of you are also wondering about this. The answer is simple. If a communication operator screws up, the officer in charge is held accountable and is subjected to court-martial. Ladies and gentlemen, the 'devil is in the details,' and nobody wants to be charged with negligence—especially since communications is so vital to the outcome of military engagements. Each of you must also strive to master administrative knowledge."

"Equipment maintenance" is exactly what it sounds like. We had to learn how to repair our own equipment. The services eliminated maintenance specialties years ago. Every operator had to do his or her own maintenance. Fortunately, most of the maintenance consisted of fault isolating using our trusty personal computer and then removing and replacing the defective part. Typically, repairing equipment consisted of accessing our computer and running the correct maintenance program. Once the computer was able to find the defective part, we would remove the bad part and install a replacement. Finally, we would run another maintenance program to ensure the equipment was operating within specifications. The tricky part was finding and replacing more than one faulty component which happened to fail at the same time. The odds of this happening in the field were slim because the individual components making up a communications system were designed with very high reliability.

Exams were really tough. Part one of our written exams consisted of answering questions relating to radio theory. We would download the quiz from the school's local area network (LAN) and prepare answers over the weekend and e-mail them to Dr. McKinnon. He would grade the exams and e-mail us the results. Part two of our written exams tested us on communication operations. Lieutenant Scott's questions were diabolical! Even with our notes and text, correctly answering her questions was challenging.

The equipment exams consisted of operating various pieces of equipment. We were required to know how to operate the entire range of communication systems. For each equipment exam we were required to set up the system within a given timeframe, transmit and receive a signal, and log off. Naturally, different levels and types of interference were added to the exercises along with built-in equipment faults. Being able to accurately receive and transmit signals through interference was the real test of a communications specialist.

Lieutenant Scott and Sergeant Newsome evaluated our performance in equipment operations and communication operations since it was impractical to separate the two subjects. Further, if we could not repair the equipment within a certain amount of time, we failed the equipment maintenance portion of our exam. Mr. Tanner was exacting in his requirements. Sometimes the communication equipment used for testing had multiple component failures, which made it especially difficult to repair.

In the evenings, Linda and I attended intelligence classes. Sergeant Braun taught us subjects such as direction finding (DF), jamming, storing, using and disposing of code keys, recording signals, and encrypting messages. He would integrate his instruction with our regular classes. This reinforced our regular classroom instruction and helped us consistently score above the ninety-eighth percentile in our regular communication class. Once, CW and Everette asked us how we were able to maintain such high grades while having to perform extra duties. My reply was that having to stay on base gave me more time for study. Linda gave a similar answer and that seemed to satisfy their curiosity.

After a short time, Linda and I began looking forward to these special classes with Sergeant Braun. Learning to intercept communications was both challenging and fun. We learned about sniffing software, decoding signals, decryption tools and techniques, and how to download intercepted signals without leaving a trace of our handiwork. Sergeant Braun was a fascinating instructor who enthralled Linda and me with his "war stories."

Our intelligence training was expanded to include covert operations. We learned techniques for breaking keypad entry devices, opening safes, conducting searches without being spotted, and other interesting techniques that might come in handy. For these classes additional faculty members would arrive on base, teach us their specialties, and quietly leave. To my knowledge, none of our classmates were even aware of their presence.

The training program took on an ominous tone as a guest instructor introduced us to Transvaal's secret corporate objectives. Linda and I listened with rapt attention to the instructor as he began outlining the corporate strategy, which was obtained by a highly placed spy within Transvaal Corporation.

"Transvaal Corporation is seeking a monopoly in the precious-metals business. Since the UAR is their largest competitor in space mining operations, we have been a target for takeover or sabotage. During the past two years, we have uncovered three separate efforts to sabotage operations at Moon Base Freedom."

"Sir, why can't we initiate a preemptive strike on their mining operations?"

"Good question, Hawkins. Any overt strike from either side would quickly escalate into an all-out war. As you may recall, we've been 'down that road' before. Both sides have to keep up appearances as non-aggressor nations; otherwise we risk widespread condemnation by other nations."

Six weeks into our training, Sergeant Braun escorted Linda and me to Captain Stevens's office. Captain Stevens asked us to sit and said, "Privates Sanchez and Hawkins, you have successfully completed phase one of your communications intelligence training. Sergeant Braun reports that you have been exceptional students. Starting tomorrow evening, you will be placed in separate training courses. Sanchez, you will attend advanced code breaking, and Hawkins, you will attend physical security. As usual, you are not authorized to share what you learn in phase two with anyone, including one another. Any questions? If not, you marines have a great evening."

On Wednesday evening, Sergeant Braun introduced me to Dr. Allen Lowman. Dr. Lowman escorted me to a private office and said, "Private Hawkins, I'm a government psychiatrist on loan from another organization. You don't need to know which organization. Tonight, I'm going to administer a series of questions in order to complete our assessment of your psychological profile. Tomorrow evening we will discuss your suitability for physical security training."

On Thursday evening, Dr. Lowman informed me of my test results. "Jim, the test you completed last night confirmed our earlier assessment of your personality. In layman's terms, you're emotionally wired to serve as a special action operative.

"What is a special action operative?"

"Jim, a special action operative is a person who can be relied upon to kill individuals designated by their agency. A soldier, in contrast, is given training on weapons usage and if required will engage and fire on the enemy. A special action operative is a little different in an important way. He's given a name and description of his target beforehand and is expected to kill that person. This is a much more personal act and relatively few people are capable of performing this task. Do you have any questions?"

After Dr. Lowman left, Captain Stevens entered the office and sat down. He looked at me and said, "Jim, now you know physical security training is a cover name for assassination training. Before you begin training, I have a nondisclosure paper for you to sign. Read it over carefully before signing. This is strictly a voluntary duty but it is the most secret duty in intelligence division."

Friday evening a nondescript man carrying a briefcase entered the room. He introduced himself as Mr. Smith as he opened his briefcase. "What I am showing you is something you must never reveal. These ten vials contain various liquids that have many uses. For example, one drop of this toxin placed on the skin causes death in fewer than thirty seconds. The biggest problem with using this is making sure you don't get any on your own skin. The next vial contains a liquid that causes temporary amnesia. These chemicals are issued in small single-dose packets for field use."

His description of each vial was clear and concise. You could tell Mr. Smith had a great deal of experience with his toolkit. I asked him why I needed this information.

"Young man, a field agent may be called upon to take action, not just report intelligence. Using these chemicals does not require brute strength. Simply squeezing a packet's content onto an opponent is all it takes to overcome a dire threat. Each agent is issued a set and is required to keep them with you on assignment. Please notice that each packet is color coded for convenience."

I was a little uncomfortable with this aspect of my job. Hopefully, I would ever have to use these chemicals on anyone.

Mr. Smith proceeded to describe the contents of each vial and ended with wishing me good luck on my assignment.

After he left, I asked Sergeant Braun, "Who is Mr. Smith?"

"He's known as 'the Chemist.' I've been told that he was once a university professor who was serving a life sentence in prison for murdering his family. One of the intelligence services got him paroled into their custody, and he's been sharing his talents with various covert organizations. It's important you keep in mind that using those chemicals has political and legal repercussions. Treat them like you would a loaded gun. The same caution will apply equally to other weapons you will be taught to use over the next six weeks."

Our morale improved, especially after our classmates began treating us more kindly. I felt like they changed from thinking of us as losers to feeling a little sorry for us. The only sore point was staying on base during the weekends while the others went into town. It was especially bad when they returned and talked about the good food and great times they'd had.

One Friday evening Linda and I were studying in our room when I had an overpowering urge to walk over and sit on her bed.

She looked up from her computer and said, "What's up, Jim?"

"Linda, do you realize we've gone through basic training together and have been roommates for several weeks and we've not really talked?"

I could see her mind working as she replied. "Yeah. I've been wondering when you would get around to this."

"What do you mean?"

"Well, it's no secret you and CW were pretty tight. Everette and

I had decided that you and CW would remain an item throughout training."

"Obviously, times change and people change. CW has had a problem with me since I failed to make KP that morning. From her recent and obvious attraction to Finnes, I guess she's written me off."

"So what am I to you, a consolation prize?"

That pissed me off, so I got off her bed and said, "Look, Sanchez, if you don't want to talk, just say so! I don't need you breaking my balls!"

Linda grinned, put aside her viewer, and said, "Whoa, amigo! I just wanted to see if you have a set of cohunes. Guess you do, after all. You know, Jim, you're the most laid-back Anglo I've ever met!"

With that said, we laughed and began getting to know one another on a personal level.

Linda said, "I'm from Lufkin, Texas. My father works on a large cattle ranch and Mother works in a factory. Like you, I decided that the military was better than ranching or working in a factory or local store."

Linda is about five feet, two inches and looks like she weighs one hundred ten pounds. She has great legs, dark hair, big brown eyes, and is really pretty. I could understand why CW had her suspicions about Linda!

We couldn't talk about our recent recruitment because the room was not secure. But I could tell she'd been going through the same hell as me. Sharing our misfortune made me realize I couldn't have had a better roommate. My opinion of Major Johnson and his recruitment strategy increased.

After a while I asked if she wanted the lights out. Linda looked quizzically at me and said, "Yeah, it's late, and I'm tired of studying." With an impish grin she added, "What else do you have in mind, Jim?"

CW was nice, but Linda was a notch above!

The remainder of our communications course seemed to fly by. Monday through Friday was crammed with classes and homework.

We even got accustomed to the long hours and lack of sleep. Linda and I spent a lot of time together on the weekends because our classmates took full advantage of their ability to leave the base. Oh well, staying behind had its rewards too. In addition to being really cute, Linda was one of the smartest people I'd ever met. Our conversations were interesting and the arguments were spirited. Getting close to her during a typical argument made the subsequent physical contact more natural and exciting. With the amount of personal contact between us, I found myself falling in love with her.

In October we were issued field jackets and gloves. Additionally, Linda and I exchanged our old uniforms for new ones. After basic training and five weeks of details at Goodfellow, our uniforms had begun to show some serious wear.

The Space Marines adopted a gray two-piece uniform made of a soft material that did not wrinkle. It can be hand- or machine-washed. As we were being issued our new uniforms, I was reminded of the differences when I was issued my uniform in basic training. This time, the clerk took pains to measure us for selecting uniforms that actually fit.

One evening as we entered our room after a long day of classes, Linda closed our door and walked up to me, threw her arms around my neck, and said, "Jim, I love you."

Oh boy. I smothered her with kisses and thanked my lucky stars for having met such a wonderful and impulsive girl. At that moment, our relationship changed from purely physical to an emotional one. This was the woman I intended to spend the remainder of my life with. Making love that evening was the beginning of something very special between us. It was better than ever before. Afterward Linda cried as we held one another. I sensed that she was as happy and content as I.

With this change in our relationship, we no longer cared about being confined to base. Linda had become the center of my life, and I hers.

On the night before graduation, Sergeant Braun congratulated Linda and me on completing our intelligence training. "I want you to know I have never taught such willing and capable marines. I would be proud to serve with you any time, any place."

He added, "Major Simpson is waiting to see you in the Commandant's office. Better not keep him waiting."

We entered his office, snapped to attention, and saluted. After returning our salute, Major Simpson asked us to be at ease and sit down. He got up from his desk and closed the office door before returning to his chair. He smiled at us and said, "Congratulations on successfully completing the communications course. You have distinguished yourselves as the top graduates in your class and have been given the highest praise by Sergeant Braun for your intelligence training. I know for a fact that he does not give praise lightly. I'm proud of you and am certain you will be very successful in the field."

"Thank you, sir," we both said.

"Yes, well, let's discuss your first mission as intelligence operatives. I don't need to remind you that this conversation is classified top secret and you must not share the details with anyone other than those designated by intelligence division."

"Yes, sir." I said. "We understand."

"First of all, you are being assigned to Moon Base Freedom."

Whoa, this was exciting and huge news! Linda and I exchanged looks and started grinning.

Major Simpson continued. "We have received reliable intelligence that a high-level manager in Transvaal has decided to send an operative to their moon base and to establish contact with one or more of our contractor personnel stationed at Moon Base Freedom. There is a strong possibility that Transvaal may again initiate trouble at our moon base. Members of our marine detachment have been placed on alert, and they have ramped up security.

"The commander of the Moon Base Freedom detachment is Lieutenant Sam Higgins. He is the only person on the moon who is cleared to discuss intelligence matters with you. However, limit your conversation with Lieutenant Higgins to operational intelligence affecting the security of the moon base. Don't reveal your training, your full mission, or any intelligence collection techniques you may use. Lieutenant Higgins is not a member of intelligence division."

The words "need to know" came to mind as Major Simpson spoke. Not even our future commanding officer was cleared to know everything about our mission!

"After arrival, you will be assigned to the communications center. You have three major responsibilities. One, help operate the commo center. Two, safeguard classified information. Three, gather intelligence and report anything that may adversely impact our mining operations."

"Sir, don't they already have a full team working commo?"

"You are correct, Sanchez. But two are scheduled to rotate out soon. Working in the commo center will be your cover. You will send and receive meteor coordinates and tracking data, meteor mining vessel communications, processed ore shipment data, and all communications between Earth and the moon, both personal and business."

"What about safeguarding classified information?"

"Safeguarding classified information are the actions you take to ensure that nobody gets access to information to which they are not entitled to know. Meteor coordinates, tracking data, frequencies, and mining vessel communications are classified secret and must be protected at all times. We've got to ensure that no unauthorized leaks occur."

"Sir, I'm guessing that anyone who can gain access to one of our meteors could steer it to a UAR population center and potentially kill millions."

"That's right, Hawkins. Losing control of an incoming meteor is one of our biggest fears."

"Sir, we're confident about being able to handle the third task," I added.

"I'm sure you will do a great job. You must review all communications between the moon and Earth. As you have been taught, someone may hide messages within routine and innocent-looking transmissions. None of the other communication operators can know that you are screening incoming and outgoing messages. They are not members of intelligence division. You must find a place to do this without letting anyone else know. Also, you will need to interview and conduct surveillance on everyone assigned to Moon Base Freedom. This includes all marines except Lieutenant Higgins. He has been vetted and cleared.

"This op order is being downloaded into your computer memory. Additionally, we are downloading personnel folders of the people assigned to Moon Base Freedom. This assignment is too important to overlook any detail."

Major Simpson continued. "You are being assigned to the moon because one, we need to replace some communications specialists who are due to rotate back to earth with their squad in a few months, and two, we've got to protect our mining operations at all costs.

"After getting back from leave, you will be given a short assignment to Fort Barrow, Alaska, where you will join a newly established squad. Naturally you are not to tell anyone about your intelligence work. Your cover for this mission is communications specialist."

Graduation from communications school was a special event. Captain Stevens and the faculty members came into our classroom. He gave a short speech and congratulated us on successfully completing the course. One by one we came forward as our names were called and had the course completion data entered on our embedded chips. Linda and I respectively placed number one and two in the class and were rewarded by applause from our classmates and the faculty members.

We were told to report to the orderly room at 0730 on Saturday morning for linen turn-in and assignment orders.

Our last night at Goodfellow was one spent celebrating our graduation. After having dinner at the mess hall, we met at the enlisted club and bought one another pitchers of beer. It was after midnight when we returned to our barracks.

Getting up at 0600 was one thing. Feeling sharp was quite another. The first sergeant had probably experienced similar occurrences. If he was disappointed in us, he hid it well. We turned in our linens and had our chips scanned. Each marine and sailor reported to Lieutenant Sinclair and received his or her assignment and travel authorization.

Linda and I were the only ones assigned to Fort Barrow, Alaska. I asked Lieutenant Sinclair if he knew anything about our assignment, but he shrugged and said no additional information on our assignment was available.

Everybody was given a three-week leave. It had been almost eight months since I had seen my parents and I was anxious to see them. On the way to the airport, Linda and I made plans to meet at the airport in Seattle en route to Fort Barrow. I wanted to hold her close before leaving, but a public display of affection between marines is not permitted. Shaking hands was not nearly enough but it would have to suffice.

CHAPTER 10
The New Job

There was no leave given when the training at al-Sidi was over. The graduates were issued new clothing to include boots and a light jacket for the trip. They also packed their space suits in special bags. After their final breakfast, a bus arrived and they were driven to the airport.

Upon arrival at the airport, they were taken to a Transvaal plane and flown to the company's launch facility.

During the long flight, Rolf noticed that his squad members were excited about the trip. Pieter and Solly sat beside one another chattering constantly while Hussein and Ibrahim couldn't stop grinning. Shanna kept her nose pressed against the window.

"Shanna, why are you looking at the clouds?" Rolf asked.

"I don't know when I will see them again. We will be gone a very long time."

"True enough." Settling back into his seat, Rolf couldn't help but think about his sorry predicament and the two long years ahead of him. He also regretted not being able to settle scores with Sergeant Hussein. There simply was not time or opportunity to give that pig what he deserved.

When they arrived at the launch facility, a bus took them to an administrative building where they were given room assignments and a schedule of upcoming activities. A pretty girl escorted them to an adjacent building containing their rooms.

Hussein and Ibrahim continuously marveled at the green vegetation planted everywhere.

"Rolf, what plants are these? I've never seen or imagined so many different plants existed," Ibrahim said.

"These are plantains, and over there are some orchids. I'm not sure about the others. I suspect they get a lot of rain at this facility each year because of this stinking heat and high humidity."

Pieter said, "Our fearless leader apparently doesn't know very much about plants, temperature, or humidity. I grew up on a farm, and this area is a veritable paradise for plants."

The girl said to Rolf, "Mr. Peters, when you have stowed your gear, please return with me to the administrative building. Mr. Leander, our station manager, wishes to see you."

After Rolf dropped his duffle bag on his bed, he followed the girl back to the office complex—not having the foggiest idea who Mr. Leander was or what he wanted.

Rolf didn't mind the office call with Mr. Leander. His office was cool, the seating comfortable, and Rolf was able to finally have a chat with someone more or less his equal. Having to endure three months of poorly educated people who could not even *spell* erudite was galling.

"Hello, Mr. Peters. My name is Steven Leander, and I want to personally welcome you to our launch facility. That desert training program was not designed for gentlemen such as yourself, but I am delighted that you graduated with no problems. We have a training program here at our launch facility for Transvaal's managers and astronauts. I have no idea why you were sent to al-Sidi. That place has a tough reputation."

Rolf knew instinctively why he had been singled out for that hellhole but chose to keep his mouth shut. No use telling everybody in the corporation that he was a "marked man" who had been demoted from the corporate fast track.

Mr. Leander continued. "Mr. Peters, there's someone from Transvaal Security who is waiting to speak with you privately. My secretary will escort you to our secure conference room. Again, congratulations and welcome to our launch facility. If there is anything I can do for you, please let me know."

Rolf was escorted into a plush conference room. As the door

opened, he saw Mr. Dieter Leher, the head of corporate security at Transvaal. Standing alongside the wall were two armed security guards.

Mr. Leher pointed to an empty seat. "Sit down, Mr. Peters. You and I have a lot to talk about."

After several long moments of silence, Mr. Leher spoke. "Mr. Peters, did you really believe you'd gotten away with murdering one of my agents? Deidre was an exceptional woman with lots of potential. She was being groomed for the most challenging and sensitive assignments. And don't bother denying it; I know you took her life."

Rolf remained silent but his heart was pounding. He began calculating the odds of killing this old fool and escaping to another country.

"You, on the other hand, have made one mistake after another. It's obvious that your engineering skills have been overshadowed by your colossal arrogance and common stupidity. According to your most recent psychological profile, you are a killer with no conscious and an inveterate liar."

Mr. Leher slid a document across the table to Rolf.

"After being shown proof of your guilt, Mr. Von Stubben signed the original of this document authorizing your execution. You can't really blame the fellow. After all, Deidre was his wife's niece!

"This signed document means I can have you shot at any time without a trial. Why don't you keep it as a reminder? I have the original in my safe."

"What proof do you have that I murdered anyone?"

"Mr. Peters, you tried erasing all evidence that Deidre had been in your apartment, but we found a trace of her blood on the carpet in the bedroom. DNA is foolproof, my boy. In addition, she placed a small marker underneath the sink in your bathroom. This is something all our agents are instructed to do. Telling me that she never visited your apartment convicted you beyond a shadow of a doubt. Before you leave, you will tell me what you did with her body. She must have a proper burial, don't you agree?"

Rolf silently folded the paper and put it in his shirt pocket.

"Mr. Peters, you owe your life to me because I persuaded Mr. Von Stubben to assign you to my department. I am keeping you alive for one reason. As one of my agents, you may yet provide a service to our company.

"Please have no misunderstanding about your future; you are no longer an engineer on the fast track to an executive position within the corporation. That part of your life is dead. You now belong to me. You have become my agent—someone expendable who possesses a background in engineering."

Rolf remained expressionless as Mr. Leher dropped this bombshell. His mind was numb and it had become difficult to breathe.

"Mr. Peters, based on your past behavior, I can't trust you to follow my instructions here or while you are on the moon. However, after a tiny device is implanted near your heart, I don't anticipate any problems with your ever disobeying or 'going rogue' on me. Your continued survival will depend on your following my every wish to the letter."

Rolf's eyes widened slightly at this news. He asked, "What kind of device?"

Mr. Leher grinned and placed a small object on the conference table. "I thought that information would get your attention. This device contains a micro-transmitter and a small vial of synthetic poison. There is no antidote for this stuff. The micro-transmitter can be activated by a special signal that will cause the vial to spill its contents into your body. Shortly afterward you will cease to exist. Incidentally, if you try to remove the device, it will automatically activate. It can only be removed by my specially trained surgical team.

"Rather than have me describe the effects of the poison, let's watch a recording of a subject being injected with this new toxin. It's amazing!"

The room dimmed as a man was projected onto one wall of the office. He was seated with his arms and feet strapped to the chair. A man dressed in a white smock approached the subject holding a syringe. He described the chemical composition of the toxin contained in the syringe and without hesitating, injected the subject. He announced the exact amount being used. The subject's body went into a brief spasm immediately followed by complete relaxation. Death was practically instantaneous. The wall went blank and the lights were turned up. Mr. Leher continued. "Mr. Peters, the transmitter will only be activated if you fail to follow my instructions. There will be no appeal or reprieve if you fail me."

"How will you know I have followed your instructions?"

"It's simple. One of my watchers will keep me informed. And before you think of finding and eliminating my watchers, please understand that they have to report to me on a periodic basis. You could say your life depends on their survival.

"Now let's get you over to the hospital and have that device implanted." Mr. Leher started laughing and continued, "It's going to make one of us feel so much better!"

CHAPTER 11
Military Leave

Returning home on military leave is a unique experience. I flew from San Angelo to Dallas to Memphis, Tennessee. After landing, I rode a train that took me to Grenada, a small city near my hometown of Houston. The bus ride from the train station was short and I arrived in the early evening.

As I walked through the streets of Houston, lights were beginning to be turned on. The temperature was cool and I was glad of the field jacket. I decided to walk home because my folks lived only four miles outside town.

Needless to say my parents were surprised to see me. I had not told them exactly when I would arrive and my mother started fussing about not being prepared for my visit. My father didn't say much, but I could tell he was happy to have me back home.

"Jim, you look so thin!"

"Well, Mom, we get plenty to eat and the food at Goodfellow Base was great! Maybe it's a combination of the uniform and daily exercise? I had gained a few extra pounds before leaving for basic training, don't you remember?"

"Son, since you are a communications expert, can you fix our video display? I have not been able to watch some of my favorite shows since we moved the projector."

"Let me take a look at it, Dad. No promises, though. They didn't teach video display repair in communications school."

We talked into the early morning hours before finally going to bed. It seemed so strange to be home. Although everything was as I had remembered, somehow it seemed different.

The next morning Dad went to work and Mom and I had a second cup of coffee. Our conversation had become more one-way since I didn't have much to say after talking so much last night.

Around 0830 I walked to town and tried locating my friends from high school. Sadly, they were either working or away at college. Houston seemed smaller and did not offer much in the way of entertainment. I returned home around noon and helped Mom in the kitchen. That afternoon, I went running. It was exhilarating to be able to run mile after mile without being tired or winded. I had never been in such good physical condition before joining the Space Marines.

At dinner, Mom and Dad carried most of the conversation. I just didn't have anything more to say. We watched the video that evening. The wireless frequency had shifted when Dad moved the unit but simple re-programming had corrected the problem. However, Dad seemed impressed with my newfound ability. There were some new programs on and Dad had his favorites that everyone was expected to watch.

On Sunday I located several of my friends and spent some time with them. Again, after a few minutes of conversation, awkward pauses occurred. I couldn't figure out why things were so different. My mother and father and my friends were the same people, only everything seemed different in ways that are difficult to describe. My friends seemed content with their lives but sounded a little jealous of my recent travel and experiences. I found I had less in common with them. It was like talking with strangers who were nice but with whom I didn't know what to talk about, especially since so much of my military life was now bound in secrecy.

The remainder of my three-week leave was spent in a similar fashion. I sat around the house in the mornings and exercised in the afternoons. Toward the end of my leave I was really anxious to get to my next assignment and spend time with Linda. I resolved to only take one week of home leave in the future.

It was not until much later that I discovered what countless military personnel throughout the centuries have also discovered.

People change after serving in the military. You change so much that you no longer have the same commonality or connection with your past. This had occurred to me, but I didn't realize it at the time. Consequently, after three days at home, I was ready to go to my next duty assignment. I was anxious to be with other marines with whom I would have something in common.

A few days before leaving home, I told Mom about Linda and showed her some pictures of us. She asked several questions about Linda's background, her family, and her religion. I answered as best I could but omitted telling Mom the exact nature of our relationship and, of course, our classified jobs. I sensed that Mom was not pleased that Linda was Hispanic and Catholic. However, she said that she would like to meet Linda someday and I took that as a possibility that she and Linda would become friends. It was hard for me to envision anyone not liking Linda.

Saying good-bye was sad. Although I was eager to start my trip to Fort Barrow and see Linda, I regretted having to say good-bye to Mom and Dad. Mom was crying and Dad was unusually quiet. After promising to write more often, I walked back to Houston and caught the bus to Grenada.

From Memphis, I flew to Chicago and then to Seattle. Linda was waiting for me at the departure gate to Fairbanks.

Being in public and remembering the rule against a public display of affection, I settled for a brotherly hug and asked, "How was your leave?"

She replied, "It was great! Everybody was the same, except my sister is going to have another baby and my oldest brother got a job with the local refinery. How was your leave? I missed you so much!"

"Other than being glad to see everyone, it was boring. And I missed you too."

Linda gave me a look like she was seeing a crazy person and said, "Boring? Jim, what's boring about being home?"

I told her about not having anything to do, how all my friends were working or at school, and how everything seemed so small.

She shook her head in amazement and said, "Mama and I never seemed to be able to stop talking. Poor Papa was hardly able to get a word in. I just don't get you, Jim Hawkins. How can spending time with your family be boring?"

Maybe I'm the one who is crazy. In any case, it was great seeing Linda again.

I let her know I had told my Mom about her. Linda was instantly curious about my Mom's reaction to the news.

"Mom would like to meet you. I'm not sure she was expecting me to fall in love with a Hispanic who happens to be Catholic, though."

Linda seemed a little miffed with that news, and I was sorry I'd even mentioned it. They say "honesty is the best policy," but they also say "silence is golden."

"Did you tell your parents about me?"

"Yes, I told them all about you, and Mama made me promise to bring you to Texas the next time we take leave."

CHAPTER 12
Fort Barrow

Linda and I managed to get adjacent seats on the flight to Fairbanks. From there we caught a commuter airline to Fort Barrow. Several other marines were also on the commuter airline, but Linda and I spent the whole trip closely huddled with one another, catching up on what we did during our leave.

As we disembarked the small plane at Fort Barrow, I immediately noticed the cold weather. It was a bone-chilling cold that set us shivering in spite of wearing field jackets. Inside the small terminal, we got our duffel bags and began looking for transportation.

A sign directed us to a military bus parked outside. The other marines joined us and we quickly boarded the bus.

It was a slow drive to the base. Fortunately, the heater was working and we were comfortable. At the gate, a guard boarded the bus and scanned our embedded chips before allowing us to proceed.

In the administrative building, we were issued cold-weather clothing: insulated boots with felt linings, face mask, goggles, sleeping bag, shovel, shelter, and other items needed for spending time in the field. It was nice not being yelled at as we stood at the counter and drew our equipment. Once again I was glad to be away from basic training. After everyone had been issued their gear, we were directed to a classroom where we received instructions on how to use the cold-weather gear and how to avoid frostbite.

During our in-processing, we met Captain Raymond DeWeiss, the Cold Weather School Commandant.

"Ladies and gentlemen, welcome to Fort Barrow. During the next three weeks, you will attend one of the most rigorous courses in the marines. You will receive refresher training in squad tactics and will have an opportunity to train as a team. The people sitting around you are the permanent members of your squad. As an added benefit, you will get acclimated to a colder environment. After this training course, all of you will know what it means to work and live in cold weather. This training will help prepare you for your next assignment."

We were directed to the mess hall where we ate dinner. Afterward we assembled in our barracks where formal introductions were made.

Corporal Hammond said, "Ladies and gentlemen, I'm very pleased to have been chosen to be your squad leader. As way of introduction, let me tell you a bit about myself. Afterward I ask that each member of our squad do the same.

"My name is Jack Hammond. I grew up in a rough neighborhood of Ontario. My father was a member of an outlaw motorcycle gang, and, I'm told, was shot and killed when a drug deal fell through. At the age of nine, my mother and I moved to Alberta where she got a job working as a waitress. After some adjustment to a new school and environment, I joined a karate club. This turned out to be one of my best decisions. Master Chen became my surrogate father, and I was never tempted to follow my natural father's footsteps into a life of crime. In fact, I earned a fourth-degree black belt in Taekwondo and represented my dojo at Olympic trials. Following basic training, I served as an embassy guard in Transvaal. Afterward I was sent to Fort Benning, Georgia, for special weapons training. My second tour was spent serving on the presidential detail in Washington DC. After that tour of duty, I was promoted to corporal and sent to leadership training at Fort Myers. Okay, enough about me; your turn."

I was impressed with CPL Hammond's background. It really helps when your leader is someone you can admire and respect. Looking around the room, I noticed that others appeared similarly impressed.

One by one the members of our squad introduced themselves.

"Hi, my name is Nora Jenkins. I'm from Ann Arbor, Michigan, and I've been trained as a medical technician. My hobbies are sky diving and fishing but not necessarily at the same time." Nora's comment was greeted with good humored laughter from all. "Oh, I'm also engaged to a wonderful man back home. He asked me to marry him while I was on leave. We plan to marry after I complete our next assignment, which will seem like an eternity for me."

"I'm Sam Higuera from Palo Alto, California. Like Nora, I am a medical technician recently graduated from the San Antonio Medical School. My hobbies are surfing and snowboarding. I am looking forward to being able to shred some slopes or surf some big waves during our next tour of duty."

"Good evening. I'm Francine Calloway from Ontario. My specialty is power generation. And my hobby is building and racing solar-powered cars. I graduated from the University of Fraser Valley and was exempted from attending technical school after marine basic training. I did get to take leave just before arriving here and want you to know that Ontario is cold too!"

"Hi. I'm Beth Joiner from Fairbanks, Alaska. I'm your friendly oxygen generation specialist and I take my job seriously. Prior to joining the marines, I attended the Alaska Vocational Technical Center at Seward where I studied power plant operations. After basic training, I completed oxygen generation specialist training at the Naval Submarine School in Connecticut. My hobbies are reading, camping, hunting, and fishing."

"Hello, Marines. My name is Frank Chen from New York City, home of the Yankees! I recently graduated from the Army's Ordnance School at Fort Lee, Virginia. My specialty is automotive mechanics to include maintaining power generation systems. My hobby is motorcycle racing and I do my own bike maintenance. I will be your other power generation specialist."

"My name is Ronald Springer. Please call me Ron. I'm from Provo, Utah. Beth and I recently completed oxygen generation training at Groton, Connecticut. My hobby is competitive shooting with high-powered rifles. I also enjoy hunting, skiing, hiking, and camping out."

"Hello. My name is Suzanne Dupree. I'm from Long Beach,

California, and am happy to be assigned to this squad. My specialties are hand-to-hand combat and weapons."

Suzanne was a beautiful woman. The male squad members exchanged looks and we gave her a loud "ooooh."

Suzanne grimaced at us and continued. "After graduating high school I learned Japanese-style Shotokan karate and have earned a third-degree black belt. After completing basic training, the marines sent me to Fort Benning, Georgia, where I received my weapons training. I enjoy going to the beach and working out. After the rude comments some of you have just made, my next hobby may be teaching you men how to show respect."

This drew a laugh from several and Frank said he wanted to be first.

Linda said, "Down, boy. I'm sure you'll get your turn at being humiliated." Then she said, "Hello, everyone; my name is Linda Sanchez and I'm from the great state of Texas! The marines noticed that I love to talk and made the logical decision of designating me as a communication specialist. I'm looking forward to many conversations and working with each of you."

That drew a big cheer from the squad. I could tell that Linda had quickly become a favorite.

Linda added, "My hobbies are reading, riding horses, cooking, and working out."

Everybody turned my way as I struggled to think of something clever to say. "Hi, ya'll. My name is Jim Hawkins and I'm from Mississippi. As you have noticed, Linda is the outgoing member of our communications team; I'm the introverted one. My hobbies are running, reading, and hiking."

The introductions being complete, Corporal Hammond said, "I want you to know that everyone here has something in common; each of you graduated in the top of his or her specialty classes! Again, I'm proud to have been chosen as your squad leader. I'm confident we will be successful in whatever the marines give us to do."

After a short bull session speculating on the upcoming three weeks of training, we turned in. I hated having to sleep alone. It had been more than three weeks since Linda and I had left Goodfellow Base, but our barracks at Fort Barrow were the open bay style (one large sleeping area), and everybody had his or her own bunk. Linda must have had similar thoughts because she gave me a wry grin and a wink as we got into our separate beds. I fell asleep thinking about how wonderful it felt holding Linda.

Our first day of training was mostly spent in the classroom. That afternoon, we took a five-mile hike to help us get acclimated to the cold and to break in our gear.

After returning to barracks, we got cleaned up for dinner.

Linda said, "Beth, I've always wanted to visit Alaska and now we're actually here! Since you're from Alaska, what's your favorite place to visit?"

"That's hard to say because there are so many beautiful sights to see. One of my favorites is Glacier Bay. I'm fascinated watching big pieces of ice break away and creating huge splashes as they fall into the sea. You see, birds feed there because the falling ice seems to bring fish near the surface. I also love Ketchikan, with its beautiful harbor and authentic Indian village. Those places are best visited during the summer."

"Why did you join the marines?" I asked.

"I was getting over a failed marriage and needed to get away and start a new life. Roy and I were just out of high school. Our marriage lasted all of six months."

"Do you mind my asking what happened?" Linda asked.

"It's been over for several months. I can't believe so much has happened since I joined the marines. Oh yeah; about Roy. I caught him cheating with another girl from our high school class. I thought she was just being friendly—hanging around our apartment and all. I guess it was only natural she and Roy began playing 'house' whenever I went to work at the restaurant."

"How did you catch them?"

"I was stripping the bed one day when I found a pair of panties that didn't belong to me. Rather than confront Roy, I borrowed a camera from a friend and set it up in the bedroom. It wasn't long before I had all the evidence I needed to get a quickie divorce and gain custody of all of our possessions, including his truck, guns, and his hunting dogs."

"That was really clever of you setting up the camera. What did you do with all that stuff?"

Beth laughed and said, "I gave power of attorney to my older sister, who hates Roy with a passion. I agreed to split everything with her fifty-fifty when she sold his stuff at auction—what was I going to do with all his junk? She told me Roy was fit to be tied when his favorite dog was sold. The Sheriff had to escort him away from the auction. I sent him a condolence card a few weeks later. I reminded him that he should have never cheated on me."

"What about the girl Roy was seeing?"

"Well, I heard that the little tramp left Roy and took up with the guy who brought his truck!"

Each day was similar to the first—a couple of hours in the classroom after breakfast and the remainder of the day spent outdoors doing heavy physical stuff.

During the first weekend, we got our gear and rations and were driven about twelve miles to a wooded area in a small valley where we set up a campsite for the weekend. This weekend gave Corporal Hammond a chance to check us out. It turned out that Joiner had the most experience with cold-weather camping. She said that her father took the family camping a few times each year during the winter. Boy, I'm glad she was in our squad. I had no problem taking advice from that woman. She really knew her wilderness survival skills.

Since there were five women and five men in our squad, Linda and I had no problem arranging to be paired in two-man tents. That evening I couldn't wait to get my arms around her.

We were picked up Sunday afternoon and driven back to the fort.

On Monday morning I got a tray of food and sat down with Ron and Frank. They were having a lively conversation about big-game hunting.

Frank said, "Man, I don't understand how you can shoot a deer even at long range. I've seen nature films of wild animals and could never understand how a hunter could take the life of an innocent animal."

Ron replied, "It's not hard. My father died and my mother became the sole breadwinner. We grew up very poor. My brother and I killed animals for food. It was either that or stand in line for government handouts. We supplemented our food by adding meat to the table."

I asked, "What is the longest shot you ever took?"

"Oh, I guess it was about five thousand feet. It was midmorning one October and there was no wind. I spotted a mule deer standing on a ridge. He was grazing when I spotted him. I didn't want to miss so I got down on the ground, laid my rifle across a rock, and aimed very carefully before firing. All it took was one shot. The hardest part was getting him back to the house. Luckily my brother was with me and he helped me bring it home."

Frank said, "I can understand your family needing food, but I don't think I could ever kill a helpless animal."

"It's amazing how hunger can change a person's priorities."

Ron looked over at me and asked, "Jim, have you ever killed an animal?"

I replied, "My family's not big on hunting. I inherited a shotgun at the age of twelve and killed a few rabbits and some quail. I guess the greatest number of animals I killed was dogs and cats."

Frank said, "Dogs and cats—are you sick?"

"No, I don't think so. In the country, some people get rid of their unwanted pets by taking them miles from home and dropping them beside the road. I guess they're hoping somebody will adopt their pet. At any rate, they get rid of their problem by dumping their animal near someone else."

"So why don't they take their pet to an animal shelter?"

"There are no animal shelters in some rural areas of our great country. In the absence of shelters, some people take their animal to the veterinarian and have them euthanized, but that costs money. Dumping is cheaper. You'd be surprised at the number of people who don't mind throwing their dog or cat out of a car."

"So how do you fit in?"

"Most people are understandably squeamish about killing pets. So when the neighbors found out about me, they would call and ask for my help."

"I know I'm going to regret asking, but what exactly did they find out about you?"

"That it doesn't bother me to kill dogs or cats."

"That's disgusting! How could you kill a helpless dog or cat?"

"It's simple; you look down the barrel and pull the trigger."

"Why would you voluntarily kill pets?"

"I figured it was more humane to kill the animal than do nothing and let it starve or get run over by a truck. On top of that, neighbors paid me to get rid of their problem. Not much but enough to buy shotgun shells plus a little extra."

"You give the impression of being this shy, introverted guy who wouldn't hurt a fly. But if you are telling the truth about killing those pets, you're one cold-bloodied SOB! I don't understand you, man."

I smiled and replied, "Well, now you boys have a dilemma. Am I a heartless son of a bitch or one of the best storytellers you'll ever meet?"

I asked Frank, "What did you do before joining the marines?"

"I worked in a clothing factory in New York. My job was cutting trouser material. It comes in huge rolls. Spreaders unroll and stack the material on large tables and automated cutting tools cut patterns of different sizes. I programmed the cutting tools."

"Why did you decide to enlist?"

"Since I couldn't afford college, I was stuck in that dead-end job. Without a degree, I could never have moved up in the company. My folks wanted more for me so I decided to join the marines and qualify for a tuition grant."

"What do you plan to study in college?"

Frank looked at me and said, "I was going to study nuclear engineering but I may change my major to communications. After all, if somebody like you can make it through communication school, it must be an easy field of study!"

I felt my face getting hot and knew my cheeks were red at being teased by Frank. He nailed me so quickly I didn't have time to retort.

Both Frank and Ron were laughing at me when Linda walked up and said, "Are you boys picking on Jim again? Hawkins is from Mississippi, and they're known for their slow-walking and slow-talking nature. Now don't confuse that with stupid—that would be a big mistake on your part. Come on, Jim. I can't ever leave you alone without you getting into trouble!"

As I meekly got up and followed Linda out of the mess hall, their laughter seemed to grow louder. At that moment I decided I had to learn how to be quicker with repartee; otherwise everyone would start calling me dumb, clod, hick, or a hundred other names.

On Monday evening the squad assembled in the gym for a workout.

"Suzanne, would you mind showing me that takedown move again—you know, the one where someone is holding a knife and coming toward you?"

"No problem, Sam. Let's get you a knife."

"I've been admiring your combat style. Don't get me wrong; I've probably watched every kung fu movie ever made, but your fighting style is way different from any I've seen."

"Sam, what you saw in the movies are staged and rehearsed combat scenes—actors and stuntmen repeating movements until they're ready for the actual filming. Real combat is nothing like the movies."

"When were you in real combat?"

"Never mind that. Here's a training knife. As you will note, the edge is blunt but the point is fairly sharp. Come at me and show me what you've got."

Sam caught the knife Suzanne tossed him and got into his best fighting crouch. He held the knife slightly in front with both elbows away from his body to help his balance.

Suzanne dropped into a crouch and kept her hands slightly in front and away from her body. She never took her eyes off Sam.

Sam made slashing movements, which Suzanne easily avoided. Suddenly he lunged with the knife. Suzanne caught Sam's wrist and pulled him toward her as she sank to the ground. Using her legs, she jammed her feet into Sam stomach as she pulled him over her body. Sam landed on the gym floor with Suzanne still holding his wrist. She quickly twisted his arm, forcing him to drop the knife.

Suzanne grabbed the knife and was on her feet before Sam could recover.

"Wow—that happened so fast. I felt like I was in slow motion compared to you."

Suzanne smiled and said, "Now you know one secret of fighting—be faster than the opponent. Often speed is the key to victory. Okay, your turn to defend against an attacker."

After repeating the exercise several times, Sam stated, "Thank you for teaching me. Suzanne, you have a lot of patience. Have you ever been a teacher?"

"Funny you should ask. Yes, I was an elementary school teacher for a year before joining the marines."

"I don't understand. You have a college degree and a great job. Why join the marines?"

"Well, that's a long story. Let's just say that joining the marines was my best option when I stopped teaching."

Later that evening, I sent an e-mail to intelligence division asking for more background on Suzanne Dupree. Specifically, what were the circumstances influencing her decision to join the marines?

CHAPTER 13
Parting is Such Sweet Sorrow

Five days later Rolf and his companions were taken to the launch pad for departure. His chest was still sore from the small incision but he was anxious to get away from Mr. Leher—as far away and as quickly as possible.

During these final days at the launch center, Rolf had been segregated from his companions and kept busy receiving various briefings on his special mission. Although the plan contained lots of pieces and players, the end result was simple—sabotage the UAR mining operations while protecting Transvaal's facility.

His final briefing by Mr. Leher gave him the latest information on the Transvaal operations on the moon. "Rolf, an insurrection at the UAR mining facility has been crushed by their security forces. Because this counts as a mission failure, I need you to replace Agent Schmidt. His ashes and a small piece of moon rock are being returned to a grieving widow."

"Normally, new employees are given a few days on our space station to acclimate to life in space, but it's urgent we get you to our moon base as quickly as possible so you can continue this critical mission. After rendezvousing with the space station, you and your companions will immediately transfer to an ore ship, which will take you to our moon base."

"Any questions?"

"No, you've made everything perfectly clear."

"Good. That's good to hear. Well, good luck, my boy. I know you're going to make us all proud."

When Rolf was reunited with the group, the inevitable question from his companions arose: "Rolf, what have you been doing all these days? We've missed you."

"Uh, nothing exciting; Transvaal has a new piece of mining equipment that more accurately assesses the quality of metals. I've been attending classes on its use and maintenance."

"Well, that knowledge should come in handy once we get on the moon."

"Yeah, I was thinking the same. What have you desert rats been doing while I was in school?"

Pieter said, "They've assigned me to work in the greenhouse at our moon base. I've been getting briefings on what plants are being grown and how to take care of them up there."

Shanna grinned and said, "They're teaching me culinary skills. I was told that with six months of studying and on-the-job training, I may qualify as a chef!"

Ibrahim looked at Rolf and said, "Hussein and I will work in metals processing. They wanted to train me in waste disposal but I refused. So Hussein and I will become metal identification specialists."

Solly quietly stated that he would maintain the water purification system.

"That sounds great. Now who's ready to leave for a cooler climate?"

Everybody replied, "I am!"

CHAPTER 14
Up, up, and Away

Rolf and his companions donned their spacesuits and rode an elevator to the top of the gantry where they slowly filed into the shuttle. Transvaal used a rocket-powered shuttle vehicle similar to ones in use by other corporations and countries.

It was obvious that this shuttle had been in service for some time. Paint was blistered in places along the outside. Inside, crates were neatly stacked from deck to ceiling.

After Rolf and his companions were seated and strapped in, he noticed that there were no empty seats. When asked, a crewmember informed him that extra seats had been removed to make room for more cargo.

"This shuttle looks like it's seen better days," Rolf said.

"Well, there is another way to look at it. This shuttle is a proven system and not likely to fail during your flight."

The hatch was closed and a deathly silence was felt until the rockets roared to life.

The flight to the space station and quick transfer to the ship taking them to the moon was uneventful. After the initial scare occurring when the rockets ignited, the trip quickly grew boring to Rolf.

Upon arrival at Transvaal Base, everybody was given an orientation briefing by Mr. Heinriks, the base manager, and was shown his or her sleeping quarters.

Rolf was appointed the quality assurance supervisor and given complete access to the facility. Shanna, Hussein, Pieter, Ibrahim, and Solly were introduced to their supervisors and given their work assignments and shift schedules.

As the orientation concluded, Mr. Heinriks said, "Mr. Peters, please come with me."

After Rolf was seated in Mr. Heinriks's office, he said, "Mr. Peters, I've been notified that you work for Mr. Leher and will report directly to him."

"That is correct."

"I have but two requirements from you. One, keep me informed of anything that will have an impact on my mining operations; and two, do not put my base or its personnel in danger. Do you understand these requirements?"

"I understand."

"Thank you, Mr. Peters. You may go."

CHAPTER 15
The Ambush

A really cold wind blew among our squad. There was no respite from the bone-chilling cold. We were betting that Captain DeWeiss had picked tonight for final maneuvers because of the forecasted low temperatures at Fort Barrow. It was minus twenty-two degrees, with a twenty mph wind blowing from the north! Our task was to move several miles inland toward an outcropping of rock and set up an ambush overlooking a road expected to be used by the enemy. The "enemy" was a platoon of Aleut Eskimos hired by Space Marines to test each squad during their arctic maneuvers.

Corporal Hammond had checked each load of his squad and briefed us before we ventured outside our warm barracks. After getting our bearings, we began the long trek to the ambush site. Noise and light discipline were in force. We were instructed to muffle equipment and cease talking. The only sound was our boots crunching on the swirling snow as we slowly made our way along the road. It was surreal in the dim light. My only view was a shadowy form in front of me and a dimly glowing, low-intensity reflective tape attached to the back of each marine's hood.

Nora was "on point," so it was her responsibility to guide the squad and alert them to enemy presence. She was equipped with a night-vision sight, compass, and a low-powered radio transmitter. Each marine in the ten-member squad was tuned to Nora's transmitter as we blindly followed the person ahead.

After thirty minutes Corporal Hammond moved up to Nora and signaled for another to take point. Frank was next in line so he took the night sight and compass from Nora, and the squad resumed moving toward our destination. Nora waited until the last member of the squad moved past before taking her position at the rear of the formation.

Each half hour Corporal Hammond would relieve the point and the squad would again move forward. After walking for about four hours, we arrived at our destination. The rocky outcrop was the first noticeable terrain feature between Fort Barrow and the Brooks Range. Our ambush site was along a series of jagged rocks ranging from fifteen to one hundred fifty feet high. A road had been built from the town of Barrow and meandered through several Eskimo villages. Part of this road ran alongside this rocky outcrop. It also provided a natural shelter from the elements.

Intelligence given to our squad indicated that an enemy patrol would be moving along the road at dawn. Our mission was to ambush the enemy and capture their vehicles and equipment. A successful ambush meant a ride back to the barracks. Failure meant having to walk back. No stronger motivation was needed as Corporal Hammond began dispersing us along a five-hundred-foot "kill zone."

As we began preparing the ambush, I couldn't help but think that this location might appear to be a potential ambush site to any halfway competent military unit. We placed training mines along the road, covered them with snow, set up our simulated antipersonnel mines along both sides of the road, and ran wires back to the rocks. Afterward we found positions within the rocks overlooking the ambush site, laid out bags containing "flash-bang grenades," and checked and covered our rifles. Our positions overlooked the road and were sheltered from the ever-present wind.

As Corporal Hammond walked by my position, I said, "Corporal, what happens if the enemy doesn't fall for this ambush?"

Hammond paused and then said, "I don't know. I'm sure other squads have used this location before. Also, our choices are limited since we didn't have time to reach another site."

This made sense to me, so I, along with the other squad members, ate food bars and settled down to await the enemy.

As dawn approached, I found myself shivering from both the cold and anticipation of the ambush. My muscles ached from maintaining a stationary position. The light was faint and our first indication of the advancing platoon was the slight noise of snowmobile engines.

As we tensed for action, several flash-bang grenades were suddenly dropped into our positions. As they exploded, I became completely disoriented and had difficulty focusing on the new threat. Evidently, so did the other members of my squad. No one had noticed a small group of Eskimos advancing on our rear. We were caught from behind and were neatly ambushed. After being utterly surprised and having our own ambush spoiled, the Eskimos gathered above us began laughing. The remainder of the Eskimo unit arrived shortly afterward on their assorted snowmobiles and snowcats.

Captain DeWeiss got out of one of the snowcats, walked over to our assembled squad, and gave us a debriefing on our failed ambush. He talked about the need for a rear guard to protect us from counter-ambush.

After collecting our equipment, we started walking back. It was a long and humiliating hike back to Fort Barrow. Nobody felt like talking so we had plenty of time to digest what had happened and how it could have been avoided. Sometimes failure can provide the best lessons.

Being assigned to the lunar colony was the primary reason for our training at Fort Barrow. Our squad would report to Base Camp Freedom on the United American Republic's portion of the moon. Temperatures at Fort Barrow simulated what we could expect at Base Camp Freedom. There was no snow or wind on the moon, but extremely low temperatures were a way of life for lunar colonists. A three-week training program at Fort Barrow gave us an opportunity to become acclimated to cold-weather operations and refresh our tactical military skills learned during twelve weeks of basic training held in a sweltering desert. A secondary reason for our training was to get to know one another. Once deployed to a contested area, our lives would literally depend upon each person in our squad. It is critical that we know and trust one another.

As I walked back to Fort Barrow, basic training seemed like a long time ago. After basic training, I was sent to a three-month communications course in Texas. This was followed by a three-week leave spent visiting my parents. Other members of my squad had similar experiences. Only Linda and I went through basic training at the same time. With the exception of Corporal Hammond, the others had gone through basic after Linda and I had. Communications training took longer to complete than other specialties.

We turned in our weapons and gear and began packing. Thankfully there was no "parade" held on our behalf.

Linda asked, "Suzanne, what got you interested in self-defense?"

"A couple of reasons, actually. My father is a policeman in Santa Barbara and my boyfriend was into karate. In fact, we'd just started dating when he earned his first-degree black belt in taekwondo."

"Are you still dating him?"

"No. He couldn't accept the fact that I was learning karate faster than him, especially since he'd started two years before me. It ended the night I won my first tournament. Guess he couldn't handle the fact that I had become better than him."

"That's so sad. A lot of men seem unable to handle a woman's success."

"Ain't that the truth!"

Captain DeWeiss entered our barracks late that afternoon, congratulated us on successfully completing the course, and gave us our orders. We were to report to Cape Canaveral, Florida. No leave en route was authorized. He also announced that Corporal Hammond would continue serving as our squad leader. We were all happy about that news. Corporal Hammond was well liked by everyone in the squad. He was a natural leader and took great pains to make everyone feel part of the team.

Captain DeWeiss added, "Ladies and gentlemen, you may be thinking that your final exercise should have ended with a victory for your side. Seldom do newly formed units such as yours win against these seasoned Eskimo troops. This is their territory and they know it like the back of their hand. Also, I want you to know that you didn't fail the training. Sure, you lost today's ambush, but you learned a valuable lesson today, one you will remember for a long time. Frankly, making you happy about your training experience was the least of my concerns. My job was to make sure you became a team and that you learned useful lessons about real combat. To that end, your unit was very successful and I would be proud to serve with you anywhere."

Captain DeWeiss entered the course completion data and authorization for transportation to Cape Canaveral on each squad members' imbedded data chip. That being done, we left the barracks and headed toward the enlisted club for beer and mutual consolation.

The enlisted club at Fort Barrow was just like every other enlisted club the world over. The only difference was size. This club could seat only twenty people comfortably. We were the only ones in the club.

Corporal Hammond bought the beer. Ron, Suzanne, and Frank did not drink beer, but Francine, Sam, Beth, and Corporal Hammond made up for them. The remainder of the squad only drank a single mug.

"Well, guys, looks like we're finally moving to our permanent duty station," Frank said. "I wonder what it's going to be like."

Corporal Hammond wryly said, "Cold."

"I'll drink to that," Francine added.

Others began laughing and talking over one another about what we might encounter on the moon. Everybody seemed really excited about the assignment.

Linda and I glanced at one another but kept our mouths shut. I couldn't help but notice that the requirement to keep secrets was becoming easier.

CHAPTER 16
Cape Canaveral

The flight to Cape Canaveral from Alaska was long. Linda and I managed to get seated together on all legs of the flight. We had a two-hour layover in Seattle and a one-hour layover in Dallas. It was late in the afternoon when we finally arrived in Florida.

Cape Canaveral is one of the oldest and best launch facilities on Earth. It's also fully equipped for training space travelers. After arrival at the "Cape," our squad was immediately sent to the training facility.

After being seated in one of the classrooms, we were addressed by the Cape's director. "Ladies and gentlemen, on behalf of our staff and faculty, I welcome you to Cape Canaveral. I am pleased that your squad is being assigned to Moon Base Freedom."

Everybody was looking at one another and grinning.

The director continued. "During the next two weeks, we will teach you everything you need to know about working and surviving in an airless environment. Please accompany the gentlemen standing in the rear, who will take you to our fitting room."

The large fitting room was staffed with a technician for each squad member. We were fitted with a spacesuit and were shown how to put on the cumbersome suit.

As we stood around in our spacesuits and adjusted the intercom sets, an instructor got everybody's attention by saying, "Okay, people, listen up. You are now wearing the Mark 19 spacesuit. It is the latest and greatest model available. I know you marines are taught that your rifle is your most important possession. Here is a new reality, boys and girls. Once you are away from Mother Earth, your spacesuit becomes your most important possession. I don't care how many guns you're carrying. Without air and protection from radiation, cold, and heat—you're dead! The Mark 19 is designed to keep you alive in an airless, high radiation, and cold or hot environment. As we proceed through the training cycle, you will find out that the Mark 19 is truly remarkable. There are only two things you must learn during the upcoming two weeks: one, how to use the Mark 19; and two, how to maintain your suit."

After removing and stowing our suits, we were driven to our barracks. They were built like an old-fashioned motel with accommodations for two people per room. Linda and I chose the first vacant room and stowed our gear before walking to the dining hall.

During dinner, Frank and Ron made some not-so-subtle references to Linda's and my room selection. There were several laughs and a few grins over their comments.

Finally, Linda stood up and looked each of them squarely in the eye and said, "Well, guys, now that you know about Jim and me, so what? If you boys need advice of a personal nature, come see me."

Both Frank and Ron sat dumbfounded, not saying anything.

Linda turned to the others and said, "Girls, keep your hands off Jim—he's mine and I don't share!" She sat down, and an uncomfortable silence followed for a few moments.

I felt my face turn several shades of red, but at the same time I was proud of Linda and in awe of her courage. The awkward silence was broken when Francine burst out laughing at Frank and Ron's blank faces, telling them they could probably benefit from Linda's advice. Conversation finally resumed but nobody had anything else to say about Linda and me as roommates. They seemed to accept us as a couple from that point forward.

Each morning at 0730 we reported to the training facility and drew our suits from the storage lockers. Typically the day would begin with a class on maintenance. I never realized that a spacesuit had so many parts! Fortunately, each of the parts had tremendous reliability, and few problems had been encountered during its extensive field use. The items requiring regular replacement were batteries and oxygen bottles.

Small rechargeable batteries powered the communication, heating and cooling, dehumidifier, and water purification modules. The communication module was identical to one Linda and I had studied. It was good to see a familiar piece of equipment.

We were discussing this when Frank exclaimed, "Hey, I was trained to repair this electrical circuit!"

Beth chimed in, "I know how to repair this oxygen system too."

After a short discussion, we realized that each member of the squad had received training on various spacesuit components. Could this be a coincidence or had someone actually engaged in a high degree of planning? In spite of my natural skepticism, I was beginning to have a greater appreciation for the person or persons responsible for putting our squad together. It didn't escape our notice that our squad was made up of pairs of marines with identical training. Redundancy improves reliability, but I hated to think about what it would be like not having Linda around.

Corporal Hammond led us in our daily physical training each morning before breakfast and classes. Cape Canaveral's temperature is pleasant during January, but our PT regimen was so rigorous that he had us sweating in no time at all. It made sense to continue working out because we would be without Earth's gravity soon, and starting our tour on the moon in great physical shape would help us in the long run.

During breakfast one morning, I sat across from Nora and said, "I need some advice."

"What is it?"

"Well, you're from a big city, and it seems to me that people from cities are better able to verbally handle themselves than people from the country. What gives you that ability?"

She smiled warmly. "I've noticed that the guys enjoy picking on you. They're like pack animals that smell weakness and take a great deal of pleasure in getting you rattled. Actually, I think it's kinda cute. You do turn several bright shades of red!"

"Yeah, well, that may be good entertainment for spectators, but I'm tired of being the butt of everyone's jokes. I want to learn how to jump back when I get trashed."

"Listen, I'm no expert on that, but it seems to me you need to do some advance planning on likely scenarios and decide what you would say during each situation. When they start teasing you next time, you'll be better prepared with a comeback. I have several cousins back home, and they really go at one another. After a while I noticed that they use variations of the same comeback. I think that after some practice, you'll get the hang of it."

"Thank you, Nora. That sounds like a great plan."

"You're welcome. I only hope I haven't created a monster!"

That evening I received the following e-mail from intelligence division answering my question about Dupree's background.

Suzanne Dupree was hired as an elementary school teacher after graduating from college. One evening after school she was sexually attacked in her classroom by two men. During the ensuing struggle, she killed both men. One of the men killed was an assistant principal named Randall Jamison and the other was a janitor named Victor Gomez—both working at the same school. Immediately after this event, the school placed her on indefinite suspension with pay. The union claimed that no teachers wanted to work with someone who had killed two of their colleagues and nobody knew if she had encouraged these men because there was no video of the incident. Because Dupree had no prior arrests, the district attorney declined to waste money prosecuting a case that would likely see her exonerated by a sympathetic jury. Relatives of one of the men killed swore vengeance at the hearing. Dupree joined the marines to get out of town. We believe that had she chosen to remain in Long Beach, it's likely she would have been killed.

I sent another e-mail requesting the names of the men's relatives.

The training at Cape Canaveral was fast-paced. After each maintenance class, we were sent to a large tank of water where we spent eight hours performing various tasks involving physical dexterity. This activity simulated working in a reduced gravity environment and gave us experience using our suits. I had to learn new techniques for walking and doing things with my hands.

After one of our training sessions in the water tank, Beth asked our dive instructor, "Sir, how is using the suit on the moon different from wearing the suit in this tank of water?"

The instructor answered, "In an airless environment, you have less resistance as you move. However, the water tank is a cheap way of introducing you to an environment with less gravity. We are unable to provide you with a completely airless environment with one fifth Earth's gravity at any training facility on Earth. However, the water tank gives you a good idea of what it's like to function on the moon. Your movements in the water are slower and require more effort. When wearing your suit on the moon, your movements will not be slowed and they will require less effort."

On the third day of our training we were introduced to acceleration and what it can do to your body. Each marine took a turn in the gravity simulator. As I was strapped in, my heart began to beat at a much higher rate of speed.

A female voice over the intercom said, "Hey, Marine, settle down. Your heart rate is pegging our meter. Relax; we haven't lost anyone in three weeks!"

I replied, "Say again the purpose of this torture?"

The voice answered, "We're going to give you some experience with the acceleration that you will find on the shuttle ride. It's better that you know what will happen rather than wait and get your first acceleration experience in the shuttle."

"Oh," I said.

I noticed that the women were called aside and a technician talked with them before they took their turns in the gravity simulator. When I got a chance, I asked Linda, "What was that about?"

She gave me a "don't be stupid" look and said, "She wanted to know if any of us was pregnant, nosy."

I reminded myself to stop being so inquisitive.

Our final exam consisted of a night march requiring us to wear our spacesuits. After dinner, Corporal Hammond called us together and gave us our operations orders. "Tonight we're going for a night march through unfamiliar terrain wearing our spacesuits. I'll send the route map to everyone's heads-up display for your own reference. Lights are useless; we'll be totally blind and must rely on the downloaded navigational map for our march. To avoid getting lost, everyone must stay linked by your ten-foot lanyard. At two reference points we will find bottles of oxygen and exchange them in the dark. We can't afford to miss any of the reference points because our oxygen bottles will only be partially filled and we must find both reference points. This final exercise will take approximately six hours. Does anybody have any questions?"

"Yeah, Corporal, why can't we just open our helmets if we run short of oxygen?"

"Glad you asked, Nora. This night march is being held off the coast of Florida between thirty and fifty feet of water!"

Francine said, "Corporal Hammond, won't there be pick-up boats with us? I mean, just in case."

"Nothing was mentioned to me about pick-up boats. I think it's safe to assume that we'll be alone during this maneuver. It's kinda like what we'll experience on the moon—I'm guessing."

Ron said, "Corporal, since Beth and I are most familiar with the oxygen bottles, I think we should check them all out at each exchange."

"Good idea. Do it. Anybody have other questions or suggestions? If not, let's go."

A bus carried us to a pier where we boarded a large work boat and headed out to sea. On the way out, we put on our suits and checked one another's readouts.

Beth noticed a problem with Suzanne's oxygen supply. After a closer inspection, she said, "Suzanne, you can't go on this dive. Your intake O-ring is damaged."

Corporal Hammond walked over and Beth showed him the damaged connection. "Corporal, the damage to this part is difficult to see and normally would have been entirely overlooked. I noticed because I heard a slight noise when Suzanne opened her oxygen. This suit can't be used until that part is replaced. Unfortunately, we don't have a spare with us."

"What could have caused this?"

"My guess, based on the reliability and the protection afforded the part, is this was no accident."

"Okay, Suzanne won't go with us, but I want this thoroughly investigated when we get back to base. Beth, I want you and Ron to double check everyone's oxygen supply. "

I overheard the conversation and quietly sent an e-mail to intelligence division letting them know of the near accident and asked them to compare the list of relatives who swore vengeance against Dupree with the names of personnel having access to Dupree's suit. If someone was trying to kill Dupree, he or she was capable of jeopardizing our entire mission.

Fortunately, with our training at Ft. Barrow and luck with the ocean floor, the remainder of the squad made the trip safely. Once ashore, we were transported back to the training area where we thoroughly cleaned and serviced our suits. Later we were driven back to our quarters and were permitted to sleep until 1000 the next morning.

At 1130, I was alerted to an incoming message. Intelligence division had found a match in the two lists of names! I was instructed to meet Major Simpson at the airport at 1500 that afternoon.

After lunch, Corporal Hammond informed us that the day was ours to spend how we chose. Because we were leaving early the next morning, we spent the remainder of the day soaking up some sun, napping, and drinking a few beers. Linda and I took full advantage of the downtime!

Around 1400 I got dressed and called a taxi for a ride to the airport. I told Linda there was something I had to do off-base and would return shortly. She wanted to come along but I made an excuse and left.

Major Simpson's flight from Washington arrived on time and we had a brief conversation near the baggage claim area.

"Jim, I'm meeting you in person because we need you to perform a difficult task. We have proof that Private Higuera deliberately sabotaged Private Dupree's air supply. We surmise his action was revenge for Dupree killing his uncle back in California."

"Sir, why not arrest Higuera for sabotage and attempted murder?"

"Normally that would be our course of action. However, his lawyer would name each squad member as a witness and that would delay your departure for the moon. We can't afford any delay in your squad's mission. There are no other marine squads ready to go in your place. In a month, we could have several squads ready but the situation on the moon has reached a critical stage."

"What's the task, sir?"

"Tonight, after everybody has turned in, I want you to give

Higuera a toxin. We need to permanently get him out of the way. Can you handle this?"

I hesitatingly replied, "Sir, I personally like Sam. He's unselfish and a hard worker. He's a friend."

"I understand, son. Unfortunately, we don't have a better option. I need to know if you can handle this."

Quietly, I replied, "I'll do it, sir but I really hate having to kill one of our own."

"I'm very sorry, Jim. This decision has been made at the very top and I'm afraid it's final. Do you have any questions? If not, I must catch the next plane back to Washington."

"No, sir. No questions."

As he started walking back to the gates, Major Simpson turned around and said, "Good luck, Jim."

"Thank you, Major."

On the way back to Cape Canaveral, I had the taxi stop at a jewelry store where I bought an engagement ring for Linda. It was a nice solitaire that cost almost all of my savings.

After returning to base, I found Linda in our room. I proposed marriage and gave her the ring. She was so excited about getting the ring that she must have shown it to every member of the squad during dinner.

After Linda fell asleep that evening, I got dressed and sneaked into Corporal Hammond's room. Both occupants were asleep. I crept over to Higuera's bed, administered a packet of toxin onto his exposed skin, and quietly left.

Back in my room, I took a sleeping pill and returned to bed. I lay down beside a sleeping Linda and spent time regretting what I had done. Even if it was necessary, I had killed one of our own squad members. Sam was a likeable guy who would be missed by his squad. I was wondering how he had arranged to be assigned to Dupree's squad when the sleeping pill kicked in.

A hand shaking my shoulder woke me. It was 0300 and few sounds were heard. The technician immediately left my room as I got up and turned on the light.

Corporal Hammond stuck his head in the room a few minutes later to make sure Linda and I were up. "Hawkins, Sanchez, let's roll."

Linda and I joined the other squad members as we walked to the bus waiting to take us to the launch pad. We hurriedly stowed our duffle bags on the bus, rode to the training facility, and drew our space suits and put them on.

Corporal Hammond asked, "Where's Higuera? Has anyone seen him?"

Shortly after a technician burst into the suit storage area and announced that Higuera had been taken to the hospital. The technician said, "I tried to wake him thinking that he had fallen asleep again when I noticed he wasn't breathing. I called an ambulance, and they took him to the hospital."

Corporal Hammond immediately called launch operations and asked for instructions. He was told that the launch could not be delayed and we must get on board.

During the trip to the launch pad, the squad members were speculating about Higuera's medical condition and were hoping that it wasn't serious and that he would join us soon. I kept my mouth shut.

As we got off the bus, Ron exclaimed, "Holy smoke, look at that monster." All of us stood gawking at the towering spaceship.

The shuttle was a large, swept-wing spacecraft with jet and rocket engines. It was standing on end and supported by three large rockets surrounded by their fuel cells. A tower gantry stood next to the shuttle. We took an elevator to the top of the gantry and entered the shuttle through a large hatch. A ladder inside the shuttle extended from the hatch down an aisle, which ran through a cramped cabin with a single row of seats on one side of the aisle. Because I was the first to enter, I took the last seat in the cabin. A large cargo compartment was open to receive our duffel bags. Each marine stowed his or her duffel bag in the compartment. A technician secured the cargo net, and each of us strapped in and plugged our suits into the onboard oxygen and communication systems. Before departing the shuttle, the technician checked everyone's harness, oxygen hose, and communication connection.

The hatch clanged shut and the locking mechanism slowly

engaged. I was very nervous as we awaited liftoff. Listening to the pilot's voice as she communicated with launch control was reassuring. However, the actual countdown was scary. "Ten, nine, eight, seven..." I was strapped in so tightly I couldn't move my head. Our communications sets were limited to receiving only. I guess nobody in the cockpit or in launch control were interested in what would have been inane chatter coming from a bunch of scared people! "Six, five, four..." Realizing I couldn't get up and leave if something bad happened gave me a feeling of claustrophobia mixed with sheer panic. "Three, two, one, *ignition and blastoff!*"

A long silence seemed to ensue until the entire ship began to shake as the rockets ignited and began to build up thrust. At first I could barely feel any movement, and then I felt my body being pressed back against the seat as the ship gained speed. The noise was deafening. My heart was doing double time for several minutes. It was a good thing our comm units had been switched to receive only. Otherwise my fellow squad members might have heard some strange noises coming from my lips. I was also grateful for the gravity familiarization training back at Cape Canaveral, though it only marginally lessened the panic building in my body.

After the shuttle reached an altitude of six miles, the primary rockets ignited in order to boost the shuttle beyond Earth's gravity and rendezvous with the space station. This time the rocket thrust was much less than we had experienced at takeoff. The flight took six hours because we'd launched at less than the optimum window. It was dark and there were no portals in the cabin so I adjusted my suit's thermostat and promptly fell asleep. The harness kept us from floating around the cabin as the shuttle flew toward our destination.

I was awakened by the noise of the shuttle's rockets burning and creating a slight force against the restraining harness as the shuttle slowed to match the space station's movement.

We'd arrived!

CHAPTER 17
Space Station A-107

After arriving at the space station, Corporal Hammond signaled us to switch on our intercom sets and get ready to disembark. We disconnected our oxygen hoses from the spaceship, connected to our own tanks, and lined up for access to the cargo container. I retrieved my duffel bag, snapped it on the suit's ten-foot lanyard, and slowly hopped over to the exit hatch. One thing I liked immediately about space travel was the fact that my duffel bag didn't weigh anything!

Since I was sitting in the rearmost seat and was first to get my bag, I was in line to be the first off. A crewmember floated over to me and said, "Okay, Marine, you get to lead the way to the space station."

There is a lot to be said for being first. First to complete the obstacle course and first in line at the mess hall are examples where you want to be first. However, being first to try something completely new and scary in front of your peers is not my favorite thing!

While training underwater at Cape Canaveral helped us navigate in a near weightless environment, there is no substitute for the real deal. I felt clumsy moving through the exit hatch. As I looked out, the space station completely filled my view. It was huge! As a kid, I'd read about it and had watched videos of its construction.

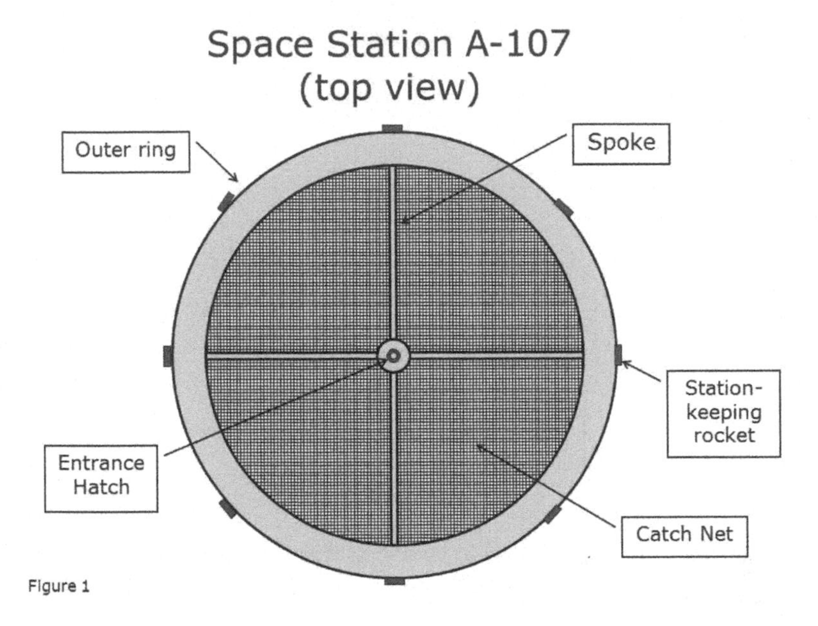

Figure 1

Space Station A-107 was shaped like a gigantic wheel. Its outer ring was held in place by four evenly spaced, cylindrical connector tubes, like the spokes on a bicycle wheel. The pressure chamber and entrance hatch were in the center. A gigantic catch net was suspended between the spokes. The station was four thousand feet in diameter and the outer ring was three hundred feet across. The station was made of carbon fiber and other synthetic materials. Its outer skin was covered with titanium sheets. It weighted three hundred fifty thousand tons and had taken seven years to build at the staggering cost of $225 billion.

Standing at the hatch exit, I suddenly noticed that our shuttle did not actually dock with the space station. A gap of at least a thousand feet down confronted me as I peered out the hatch. I looked down and saw nothing below my feet. My balls seemed to shrink up into my abdomen and I quickly tightened my grip on the edges of the hatch exit and pushed back into the shuttle to keep from falling.

My buddies took delight in giving me suggestions as I slowly began leaning out the exit hatch. "Come on, Hawkins, show us the way! We're counting on you to make us proud.

"What do you see?"

"What are you waiting for?"

"Come on, Jim, we need to use the head!"

A crewmember, attached by a lanyard clipped to an eyebolt on the outer hull of the shuttle, said with a grin, "Don't worry, mate, I'll give you a shove and all you have to do is catch the net anchored to the space station. We haven't lost anybody in more than six months."

I asked him, "Why doesn't the pilot land on the space station?" He replied, "Sorry, we don't dock the shuttle to the space station. That's only done in science fiction movies. This procedure saves us fuel, time, and reduces wear and tear on the equipment."

I wanted to ask more questions, partly out of curiosity but mainly to delay what was coming, but he grabbed my arm, jerked me away from the hatch, and launched me across the void to the space station. As I traveled away from the safety of the shuttle, I felt a slight jerk on the lanyard and noticed that my duffle bag was following me like a faithful dog. Unfortunately, the momentum of the duffle bag was enough to cause me to begin a slow cartwheel as I and my duffle bag slowly moved toward the net.

Relief was seeing the catch net looming larger and larger each time it came into my view. After a surprisingly soft impact against the net, my body began to slow and I grabbed some strands of the net to keep from rebounding. Nothing ever felt as good as holding on to that net and knowing that I was relatively safe and not going to fall back to Earth. I slowly made my way across the net to the open hatch.

I could hear my buddies laughing and making rude jokes about my landing. I was thankful I had been able to suppress a scream of terror as I cartwheeled through space.

As I reached the entrance hatch, I turned around to see the other members of the squad moving toward the net. There was a wide gap between Springer and Chen. I suspected Chen had been reluctant to make the trip. Oh boy, would he get ribbed once we were all inside!

"Yee haw!" There was no mistaking Corporal Hammond's shout as he hit the cargo net.

When the last of our squad was safely aboard the space station, the entrance hatch was closed and the room pressurized. After the pressure had built up, a lit sign indicated that was safe to move from the pressure chamber into the corridor. Once in the corridor, we promptly removed our helmets and looked around.

As we exited from the pressure chamber to the hub, I noticed a line of five suited men waiting to enter the pressure chamber for transfer to the shuttle. Space Marines stood with weapons drawn at both ends of the line. They were a grim-faced bunch of people inside the helmets who didn't speak as they silently moved into the pressure chamber.

A small amount of gravity was present in the space station's hub. When I asked a space technician, he informed us that even more gravity is present in the outer rim. In fact, the gravity in the outer rim is one fifth that of "Earth normal."

To move from the hub into the outer rim, we took one of four elevators running the length of the spokes of the space station. As we neared the outer rim, the amount of gravity pulling us "down" noticeably increased. The elevator stopped on the second floor and we were shown to our rooms. Our first task was to remove our space suits and place them on special hangers located near the door.

Each room contained a lit schematic of the station with a "you are here" highlighted on each drawing. Navigation was easy even though the station was extremely large and contained numerous corridors and rooms. Because this was our first time to ever visit a space station, we were curious about its layout.

Corporal Hammond gathered us in the hallway and said, "Split up and conduct a recon of the station. Report back here in forty-five minutes. Use your video recorders and we will review them later. I have to report to the station commander and check in."

Linda and I scouted the first floor. On the first floor (upper storage area), we discovered a vegetable garden spread out among thousands of crates. The garden used hydroponics as its main growth medium. Several contractors were tending the garden. We were informed that it grew all the vegetables consumed on the space station. This reduced the amount of food shipped from Earth. It also saved space on the shuttle for other items.

Suzanne took the second floor, Nora the third, Frank and Ron the fourth, and Francine and Beth the fifth floor, or lower storage area. Later, when we assembled in a conference room, images from our video recorders were projected on the wall.

The squad members reported the following information. Living and storage compartments were part of the outer ring. There were three main decks and huge storage areas on "top" and "beneath" the main decks. The mass contained within these storage areas help block radiation from the living quarters.

The station spins slowly in a clockwise motion. This builds up centripetal force that simulates gravity. Naturally, the force is strongest in the ring because it is moving faster than the hub. Eight large rockets evenly spaced along the outer ring provide the spinning force. Due to the rotation and gravity, the sensation of "up" is toward the hub of the station. Every seven days, the rockets are ignited for about twenty minutes. This small amount of thrust each week is enough to maintain rotation and keep the space station at a constant distance from Earth.

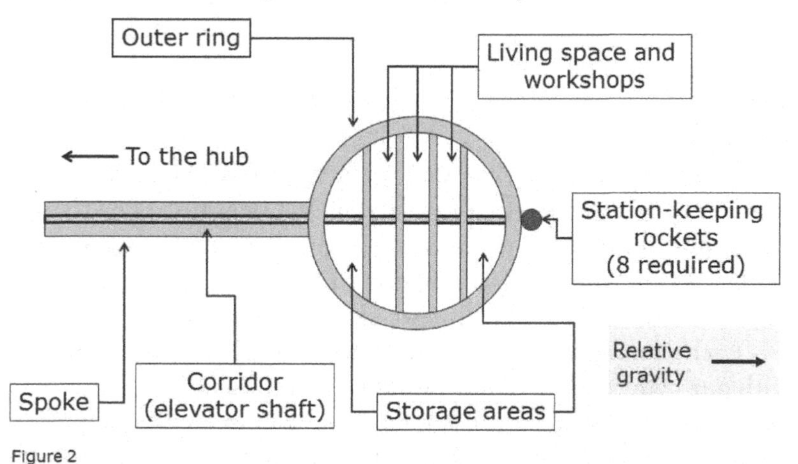

Figure 2

Station A-107 is owned and managed by the UAR. It serves as a waypoint between Earth and the moon. Although vital as a transit point for personnel, another purpose served by the station is to repair and refuel the spaceships that shuttle to the moon and back. Fuel for trips to the moon is siphoned from the space shuttle and stored in a container located about 3 miles from the space station.

We discovered that a large percentage of the station is devoted to logistics operations. Approximately one hundred twenty civilian technicians provide staffing. Their jobs are moving cargo, performing maintenance, and doing housekeeping tasks, such as preparing meals, cleaning, operating the waste disposal and water purification units, tending the garden, processing food, and staffing a small hospital. Security is the responsibility of a forty-two man platoon of Space Marines. A contingent of twenty-five navy personnel performs station-keeping tasks. These encompass maintaining a geosynchronous orbit around Earth, station rotation to maintain the artificial gravity, overseeing docking operations, and operating the communication system. A navy captain commands the space station. Everybody is very busy and the staff doesn't have much free time. Staffing is held to a minimum in order to reduce overhead costs.

The European Union and two mega-corporations (Comtec and Transvaal) maintain their own space stations in geosynchronous orbit around Earth. Each has a similar design and serves a similar purpose. The days of sharing a space station with other nations are long gone.

Corporal Hammond thanked us for the information briefings and informed us that we would be here for eight Earth days waiting for the moon shuttle.

Hurry up and wait! It doesn't matter how many times you experience waiting, it never gets easier. While waiting for the ship that would take us to the moon, Corporal Hammond scheduled drills in using and maintaining our suits in addition to practicing hand-to-hand combat in a near-weightless environment.

Each evening Linda and I managed to find time to experiment with our own version of "near-weightless training."

One squad from the marine platoon volunteered to help us get acclimated to near-weightless combat. The hand-to-hand training took place in a room about the size of a racquetball court, with padding along the walls.

One by one they beat us in one-on-one combat. There are a lot of techniques used in space that are impossible on Earth. They were able to better gauge how far they could jump, how to use one hand for a takedown when using two was normal back on earth, etc.

Getting beaten by those marines motivated us to learn and adopt their strategy.

Our first victory was attained by Suzanne. She faced a cocky marine who boasted that no woman could put him down! Suzanne was not just an attractive woman; she was solid muscle and an expert in hand-to-hand combat. She didn't raise her voice; she smiled and asked her challenger if he had always been a "mama's boy." The overanxious marine rushed her, but she was ready for his lunge and quickly stepped aside and grabbed his arm as he raced past. She used his own momentum to flip him against a wall and then jumped on his back and twisted his arm until he yelped in pain. The short fight was stopped shortly afterward with Suzanne being declared the winner.

After the individual contests were over, the victorious marine squad left the training room and headed to the bar for their victory celebration. Corporal Hammond and Suzanne began teaching us some moves that had not been covered during basic training. We began getting better and it wasn't long before we could hold our own with the other marines. Over dinner one evening, we were informed that the squad that volunteered to spar with us was the station's champion team. That fact made us feel even more confident in our ability to fight.

As an added bonus during our stay at the station, we drew weapons from the station's armory. Each weapon was electronically coded to an individual marine. Nobody else could fire your weapon until the armorer changed the weapon's access code. This might sound like a risky policy—no longer could you pick up a buddy's weapon and continue the fight. On the positive side, neither could the enemy!

I asked Suzanne, "What is the range of these weapons?"

She laughed and said, "In space, a projectile goes until it hits something. On the moon, the maximum effective range of this weapon is greater than you can see. So be careful where you point that thing." That comment drew a laugh from everybody and caused me to blush.

One of the maintenance shops in the space station doubled as a firing range. We spent hours and hours practicing with weapon simulators. Corporal Hammond told us that we would take our new weapons to the moon.

Our weapons were radically different from traditional firearms used on Earth. For one thing, gunpowder does not work in space or on the moon because gunpowder requires oxygen and a flame to ignite (explode). Our weapons fired (or launched) small rockets. These tiny rockets are accurate over great distances if they are fitted with a heat seeker. The heat-seeking device in the bullet directed the round to the nearest heat source within a certain radius. Not surprisingly, all space suits radiate heat. In an airless environment, you don't have to actually hit the person, just make a big hole in his or her suit. The lack of atmosphere will do the rest. This is referred to as a "secondary catastrophic effect."

For close-up work, our weapons also fired a projectile that contained eight stainless steel darts. Each dart was about the size of a six-penny finish nail with tiny fins crimped on one end. The proper name was a "fléchette." This ammunition was preferred for use inside a building. Once fired, the darts would separate and form a circular pattern about the size of a dinner plate. Around thirty feet the darts formed a looser pattern about seven feet squared. Your odds of hitting a moving target at short range increased significantly.

Since we had never used these weapons, learning how to fire them and improving our accuracy was a top priority. Each weapon was fitted with a laser device that was used in lieu of firing live ammo. This saved money and allowed us to really become adept with the new weapon. The circumstances were different too. I didn't have Sergeant Hernandez standing over me yelling about my lack of known parents. Our squad, to a marine, readily adapted to the new weapon. I was proud to be a member of this unit.

Everyone was impressed with Ron's exceptional shooting skills. I remembered his comment about enjoying long-range shooting. Corporal Hammond designated him as our squad marksman.

Dying is never pleasant, but our profession is to make the enemy die for his side. This requires practice, practice, and more practice.

CHAPTER 18
Final Destination

Although the people aboard the space station were friendly and the food great, it was good news when we heard that a ship was docking at the station and that it would take us to the moon. We were anxious to get to our first real assignment.

Corporal Hammond briefed the squad on our mission. "Listen up; I've received our orders. Our job will be to augment security at Base Camp Freedom. Specifically, some of the contractor personnel were caught planting explosives in the power generation station while others attacked the comm center. Remember seeing those civilians leaving the station as we arrived? Well, those sterling individuals were being sent back to the UAR for trial and their just rewards for attempted sabotage and murder. At any rate, we're going to be spread real thin on the moon. At Base Camp Freedom, there is a marine detachment made up of three squads. The detachment is commanded by Lieutenant Roger Higgins. That means only three squads are protecting the moon base and its mining operations. We are replacing one squad, which is past due for relief.

"According to a message I received from Moon Base Freedom, Lieutenant Higgins has already given us our assignments. After arrival, seven of us will divide into two teams and secure the dispensary and barracks while his two squads secure the remainder of the moon base. Hawkins and Sanchez, you rotate communication duty. The commo specialists assigned to the other squads were killed during the revolt, which means you two are the detachment's only communication experts. With only three squads available to secure the moon base, this will mean a six-on and six-off duty cycle until relieved."

"Corporal, why don't they send more marines to better secure the facility?"

"Good question, Calloway. The brass believes the situation is temporary and they don't want to spend the additional money for more overhead cost. It's up to us to prove them right."

Jenkins asked, "What about sending one of the squads from this space station to reinforce Moon Base Freedom?"

"According to the station commander, he can't reduce the strength on his station. From simulated war games and from the latest intelligence, our leaders have concluded that this station is being manned at a minimal level for its own safety. The station commander added that if they reduced the forces here, unfriendly governments from other space stations could launch a sneak assault on this station and take it over before we could get reinforcements up from Earth. Can you imagine how many lives would be lost if we were forced to assault this station directly from an earth-launched space shuttle? Any earth-launched mission cannot be done secretly, that's for sure! Casualties would exceed 75 percent, with no guarantee of mission success.

"I have other sad news for you. I have been informed that Private Sam Higuera did not make it. The hospital reported that he died of heart failure. They think the stress of the mission and impending launch were the triggers for his heart attack. I was told that Higuera's replacement has been designated and he may arrive on the next shuttle from Earth."

"Nobody knew he had a weak heart?"

"I'm sorry, Nora. His heart condition was not detected, nor was it mentioned in his medical records. I've heard of cases where people go through life not knowing they have a weak heart."

I inwardly breathed a sigh of relief when I heard this news. Apparently, my action had gone undetected. I fervently hoped I would never be required to do anything like that again.

Frank asked, "Corporal, you mentioned 'until relieved.' What does that mean?"

"I don't know for sure, Frank. The Lieutenant didn't say. However, since we are the new squad, I'm guessing we'll be the last squad to be relieved. Besides, isn't this operation what you signed up for? I know duty on Moon Base Freedom would always be my first choice."

Not much point in arguing that one. Adventure, "seeking the unknown" is why each of us joined the marines.

"Okay, let's get down to business. Look at the vid screen. Here is a layout of the moon base facilities. Sanchez, Hawkins, I'm giving you a data disc containing this stuff. Download the schematics and maps onto your computers. You can also download a video file that will take us through the entire facility on a virtual tour. I want you to show the layout and video tour to every member of our squad and as many times as they need to see it during the next six days.

"People, memorize the facility during our six-day trip to the moon because we won't have time for the grand tour or customary in-processing when we arrive. The squad we're relieving will rotate out just as we arrive. My advice is to get plenty of rest during the final leg of our trip. It looks like we're gonna need it."

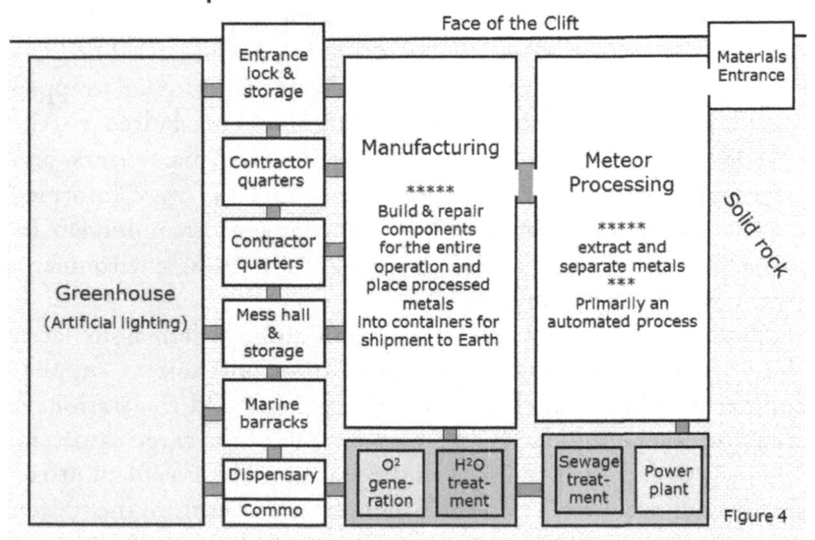

Figure 4

Linda and I had our own orders concerning our mission. Supplemental orders had arrived via an encrypted e-mail. They contained the latest intelligence on the personnel living at Base Camp Freedom. Individuals with known or suspected sympathies to mega-corporations had been identified. We would be required to track their movements in particular. Simply stated, we had to accomplish this additional job without anyone's knowledge. This included our fellow squad members.

On a few occasions, Linda and I were able to discuss our special assignment with one another. Finding a secure place for communicating was challenging. We discovered the best place to talk about classified subjects was to get on a bed and cover up with a blanket. Ensuring that our personal computers were offline, we typed comments and questions for each to see. After, we erased the chat room memory on the computers.

A klaxon sounded throughout the space station announcing the arrival of the moon ship. Its name was Jupiter 1-C. Our squad gathered in the observation room in order to see the ship as it drew closer to the space station.

Jupiter 1-C was the epitome of utilitarian. It wasn't streamlined and I doubt it had ever been painted. Long grayish-black streaks covered the dented exterior. So much for aesthetics! The ship consisted of six large cargo cylinders and one fuel cylinder strapped together and surrounded by three large rockets bolted to the cylinders. A box-like container housing the crew, passengers, and instruments was mounted on top of the ship. We were informed that the configuration of the ship would change to accommodate its cargo. Further, since it always operated in an airless environment, streamlining was not an issue.

Jupiter 1-C docked near the station about a half hour later. We watched from the station's observation porthole as supplies and personnel shuttled between the cargo ship and the station. A crewman on the ship fastened cables on each of the cargo canisters. A winch pulled each canister to the station. The crewman at the ship used another cable to quickly move small boxes from the station to an empty container on the ship. The bands holding the engines tightened on the reduced number of containers. The engines were repositioned for even spacing.

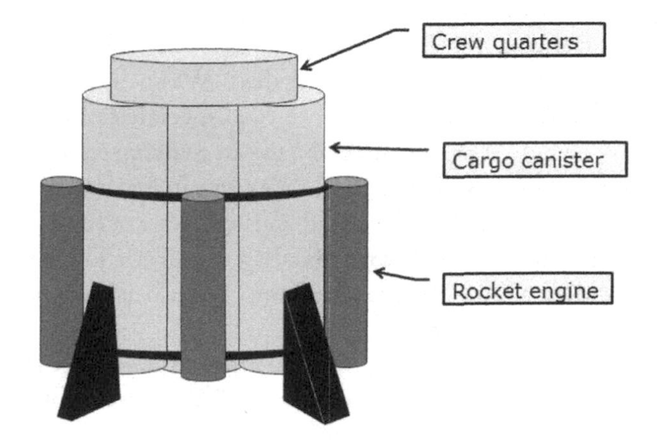

Figure 3

Our turn to suit up and embark came without a lot of fanfare. The off-duty marines stopped by to wish us well.

The station crewmember snapped my suit to the cable and helped me push away from the station across the void to the ship. The crewmember aboard the ship unsnapped my suit and directed me inside the airlock. Three people could enter and exit the airlock at a time. Since precious oxygen was lost with each cycle, I had to wait until Frank and Francine arrived before cycling the airlock.

After exiting the airlock and entering the crew accommodations, I opened my helmet and was almost overwhelmed by the stench of unwashed body odor. The place stank to high heaven. Francine started gagging. The captain, strapped in his command seat, laughed at our obvious discomfort and said that we would get used to the smell, especially since there was no shower facility on board. John wryly observed that we couldn't step out for a breath of fresh air.

The remainder of our squad was quickly transferred and the cables released. Jupiter 1-C shifted to the refueling point and completed its preparation for the return voyage. The first officer informed us that we would be weightless during a majority of our trip to the moon.

Unloading and loading the cargo ship took less than one hour to complete. I could tell that the crew and technicians knew their jobs and had done this many times.

Our six-day trip to the moon was long and uneventful. After experiencing a slight acceleration for the first day, we were in total weightlessness for the next four days. We spent our time talking with one another, reviewing our technical specialties, and memorizing the base layout. Working out was limited to using rubber bands attached to handholds along the walls. We slept in mesh hammocks that were strung between the deck and ceiling. We ate food out of a squeeze bottle, and the single toilet facility was crude but efficient. My only comment about life aboard Jupiter 1-C is, "Inside is marginally better than being outside!"

During the days of having nothing to do, we prevailed on Corporal Hammond to share his knowledge of world events with us. Ron said, "Corporal Hammond, you've been assigned to embassy duty and had a tour as a member of the presidential detail. I'm sure you have been exposed to loads of diplomatic speeches and conversations. Can you tell us what started this latest contest between the UAR and Transvaal?"

"You're asking a question that has multiple answers. For example, you could ask this question in the European Union, in Comtec, UAR, and Transvaal and would get four different answers."

"My best answer is, our government's biggest nightmare is that the mega-corporations will gain control of our own domestic businesses, which will start the process of assuming control of our government. Business is their reason for existence. Increasing their corporate wealth is their goal. Mega-corporations continue to maintain large armies of well-equipped mercenaries to protect their gains.

"As you can imagine, the remaining governments exercise a great deal of control over trade between their domestic corporations and these mega-corporations. Government officials are paranoid about free trade with the mega-corporations. This is especially critical since many of Earth's natural resources are almost depleted.

"Due to international treaties governing which weapons are permitted in space, combat ships and selected munitions are forbidden. Up here, Space Marines and Transvaal mercenaries are only equipped with small arms. This is why we don't have access to any heavy stuff up here."

Nora said, "Geeze Louise, Corporal that sounds complicated. My high school teacher tried to make me understand this subject, but I wasn't interested at the time. Today is different. I'm trying hard to understand but it still sounds like no solution is on the horizon."

"You're right; no permanent solution. But our job is to make sure any temporary solution works to our nation's best interest."

Two days before arrival we began receiving more frequent transmissions from the moon. Lieutenant Higgins gave Corporal Hammond updates of the situation on Base Camp Freedom. We also received news from Earth. The relations between the mega-corporations and the nations were more tense than normal. The mega-corporations were arguing that the 1967 treaty keeping the moon and other heavenly bodies independent of all nations did not apply to them since they were not considered national entities and did not participate in the treaty. Leaders on all sides were trying not to be the first to blink.

The UAR was deeply involved in trying to maintain agreement among allied and neutral nations against the united front presented by the mega corporations. Sometimes it seemed that the UAR was alone in these diplomatic bouts. Nonaligned nations were mostly content to sit on the sidelines and await the outcome. The European Union and Indian Republics were our strongest allies in these diplomatic contests. The Islamic Republics and Republic of China seemed to delight in playing one side against another.

I was certain the reason for the increased tension back on Earth had something to do with our marines having a shootout with the terrorists.

The captain announced that he was starting the deceleration cycle and would land on the dark side of the moon.

"Why are we landing on the side away from Earth? I was hoping to wake up every morning and see something familiar."

"Well, sonny, somebody was afraid that one of our meteors being harvested might crash on Earth instead of the moon. Let's just say that most folks don't care what we do as long as we provide a continuing supply of raw materials."

Beth asked, "What's the problem of guiding the meteors to a deserted spot on Earth and processing the meteors at home?"

"There are two problems with that option, missy. One, some meteors are really big. Their impact on Earth would throw clouds of dust into the upper atmosphere and cover thousands of miles. Environmental impact on our weather could be severe. Two, people are afraid that a stray meteor could hit their hometown and blast it to kingdom come. Hell, the environmentalists are happy because 'out of sight, out of mind.' I've even heard that some wacky astronomers are claiming that our mining operations are slowing the moon's separation from its Earth orbit! I say, 'Whatever floats your boat.'"

"Aren't there dust clouds on the moon?"

"You betcha; there are some large ones too. But remember, it's an airless environment and there are no winds to blow the dust. It eventually falls back to the moon's surface. However, right after an impact, it's especially hard to see if you are in the impact area."

Twenty-three and a half hours later, the ship was inverted and all rockets were ignited. We felt ourselves pushed into our seats as the ship slowed and then bumped to a stop.

CHAPTER 19
Guard Duty

Our landing at Base Camp Freedom was smooth. We suited up, grabbed our duffel bags and weapons, and exited the freighter. Here on the moon my duffel bag was very light and really easy to manage. What weighs two hundred pounds on Earth only weighs thirty-six pounds on the moon—about six times lighter! The crew disembarked and led us to the entrance. I noticed that my boots sank into four inches of dust as I stood on the moon. The dust was everywhere.

I asked, "Why is there so much dust?"

The captain replied, "We're a few feet away from the meteor impact zone. Over time, the striking meteors have ground the moon rock in the impact area into a thick layer of dust, which has scattered beyond the immediate impact area."

The landing pad and launch platform was located about a thousand feet from the meteor processing entrance to the moon base. However, we walked at least twenty-three hundred feet along the bottom of a sheer rock face in order to reach the main entrance of the moon base. We quickly discovered the best means of walking on the moon's surface in a bulky space suit. "Take short hops—they really move you along." I thought back to the recent training at Cape Canaveral and silently agreed with whomever had given that advice.

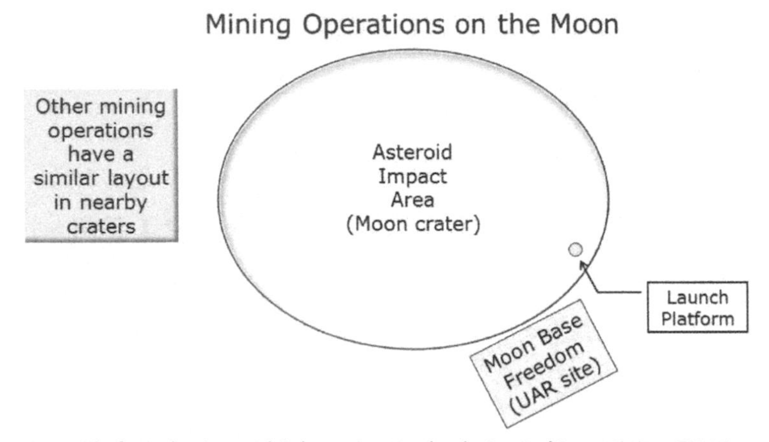

Asteroids from the Asteroid Belt are sent to the designated impact area. Entering and retrieving asteroids (now called meteors) from the impact area is dangerous work. Once retrieved, meteors are processed at Moon Base Freedom into raw materials before being sent to Earth. Waste material from each meteor is dumped in the impact area.

Figure 6

I noticed that the entire base was built into the face of a rock cliff. That gave me a feeling that we would be well protected from radiation and the occasional meteor strikes. The only manmade things visible from outside our moon base were the two entrances.

The entire squad jumped after we felt a strong tremor. It seemed to originate to the right of us. Turning, I saw a huge geyser of grayish-black dust erupting into the air.

The crewman leading us to the base laughed and said, "Don't worry, lads; it's just a small meteor landing in the impact area. A retrieval crew will be out shortly to bring it in for processing. This happens continuously. You'll soon get used to it."

I noticed that the dust cloud hung suspended in the low moon gravity for a long time before slowly falling back to the surface. Due to the low gravity, it would take a lot longer for the dust cloud to clear than it would have in Earth gravity.

After we entered the decompression lock and the outside door closed behind us, a loud noise began. I felt my suit being buffeted by a swirling wind. The dust that had collected on our suits was being vacuumed and exhausted into a large grating in the deck. After a couple of minutes, I heard a loud clang and then the now familiar and welcoming hissing of air entered the decompression lock. Looking around, I saw a crewmember from Jupiter 1-C operate some switches located on the wall. He was manually operating the decontamination and decompression steps.

First Sergeant Barnett was on hand to greet us as we exited the decompression lock and walked into the entrance foyer.

After we removed our helmets, First Sergeant Barnett said, "Welcome to Base Camp Freedom! I'm really glad to see you, marines. Lieutenant Higgins wants to talk with you before you go on duty. Please remove your suits and stow your duffel bags in the barracks. Your names have been placed on your bunks and lockers. We'll meet in the conference room in ten minutes. It's on the right down this corridor."

The entrance foyer was large, well-lit, and painted a bright color. A main corridor ran through the personnel portion of the base and connected several large chambers. Each chamber was subdivided into a number of individual rooms. There were airtight doors spaced along the corridor about one hundred fifty feet apart.

First Sergeant Barnett continued, "These doors are closed any time an atmospheric breach in the base occurs. You need to get to the nearest air station and put on a mask until the breach is sealed or until you can get to your suit. The mask is equipped with a small oxygen bottle that will give you twenty minutes of air. I don't have to tell you that should we have a breach, speed is essential."

As we walked down the hall, some marines passed us as they moved toward the decompression lock in single file. Even though they were in their space suits, you could tell they were tired by the way they walked. Three marines were carrying the fourth on a stretcher. If this was the squad we were replacing, they were missing six members.

Inside the conference room, we were told to be seated.

When Lieutenant Higgins entered the conference room, Corporal Hammond stood up and said, "*Squad, attention!*"

"*At ease and take your seats,*" Lieutenant Higgins said. "Ladies and gentlemen, I want to add my own welcome to the one given to you by First Sergeant Barnett. Corporal Hammond, I assume your squad is ready for duty?"

"*Yes, sir!*"

"That's great. I apologize for the lack of ceremony to celebrate your arrival, but you've got some work to do. As our newest arrival, I am designating you as third squad. Corporal, post four members to guard your assigned areas, and you and the remainder follow First Sergeant Barnett. Hawkins and Sanchez, kindly follow me. That's it for now—*squad, dismissed!*"

Linda and I accompanied Lieutenant Higgins into his office. After closing the door, he asked us to be at ease and take a seat.

"Six marines have been killed. Their cremated remains are being transported home along with four marines who have been assigned convalescent leave.

"Two weeks ago, one of the rogue contractors broke into the communications room and surprised our entire commo team. The team had gone without sleep for a couple of days and momentarily let their guard down. The attack cost us six marines who were our only communications experts in the detachment. I don't know why the attacker chose the comm room. We searched his body and belongings but didn't find anything out of the ordinary. Since that attack, First Sergeant Barnett and I have been taking turns monitoring the radio equipment since the loss of our commo team. Fortunately, none of the settings was changed, and we have been receiving meteors on a normal basis.

"We killed three and arrested five of the terrorists who were involved in attacking my marines. But I don't know if we got them all. You need to be careful, stay alert, and don't trust any of the civilians. Got it?"

In unison we said, "*Yes, sir!*"

"It's a relief to have you two on board. I'm aware that you also have a classified mission and you have a free hand and my full support to complete your work. Regarding communication operations, I'm afraid there is a lot of administrative stuff to clear up. We got way behind."

Linda replied, "No problem, sir. We can handle it."

"Your first priority is to check the coordinates of the incoming asteroids. Our mining operations are wholly dependent on sending and receiving accurate navigation and landing data. Make sure the landing party knows when to expect each asteroid. All incoming asteroids should be programmed to hit the impact area. The exact time of impact is the only way our guys know when it's safe to enter the impact area. Our next asteroid will impact in four hours and forty-five minutes. If you have questions, call me on my private channel." He added, "I haven't slept in more than forty-eight hours and need some shut eye before the shift changes."

Linda and I left for the communications room and took a quick inventory. There were three entrances into the dispensary but only one entrance from the dispensary into the communications center. I locked the comm center door and we loaded our weapons and placed them nearby, just in case.

The communications equipment seemed to be in good shape and was operating satisfactorily, but the lieutenant was right—a lot of catch-up administrative work was needed. I guess the lieutenant and first sergeant had a lot of other stuff to do, especially after losing six marines!

"Jim, do you want to handle the message traffic or do paperwork?"

"I don't care. You choose. It looks like there's plenty of work to go around."

I spotted a disc lying in the corner of the commo room. "What's this disc? Are we supposed to load this into the computer? There's no label."

"I wouldn't do that. There's a possibility that the disc was dropped by the same guy who was killed while trying to gain access to the commo center. If we loaded that disc, it's possible we could be completing his mission for him."

"Yeah, you're right. If it contains bogus coordinates, a year's supply of meteors could be sent elsewhere. And that's not all. This disc could even contain new coding for our mining ships. New codes, if sent by our secure transmitter, could direct our mining ships and robots to obey instructions from another source. In effect, the UAR would lose all of its mining ships."

Linda grinned and said, "Be careful which slot you put that thing in—referring to the disc, of course."

Instead of trying to analyze the contents of the disc, I placed it in a special container and addressed it to an innocuous location in Washington DC. It would be carried by the next ship to our space station and then onward to Earth for delivery to the special address. Someone from intelligence division would get the pleasure of analyzing its contents. We already had too much to do just getting the communication operations back on a smooth track.

"Okay, boss lady, what do you want me to do?"

"Help me check the meteor coordinates to ensure they remain on their programmed course and schedule. Once that's complete, you can run diagnostics on each mining vessel to verify their operational status while I catch up on the message traffic. There's a lot of incoming and outgoing stuff in the queue. Resuming normal traffic will send a positive signal to everyone that we have things under control at Moon Base Freedom."

Communication operations and guard duty quickly became routine, more or less. Linda and I took turns visiting other parts of the moon base while we were not on commo duty. This cut into our sleep cycle because there were only two of us to man the communication equipment. After each walking tour, we would immediately debrief the other so we were kept fully aware of the situation. On a personal note, the shift work gave us no time together, and that really sucked.

We received an average of fifteen messages from Earth per shift. Each message had to be screened before we forwarded it to its recipient. We were determined that no unauthorized message traffic to corporate traitors would pass through our commo center.

Personal messages intended for marines and contractor personnel were forwarded to a public message console located in the dining room. The screen would list names of those with messages waiting. By using their personal identification codes, messages could only be read by its intended recipient. This same console was used to send personal messages back to Earth. Naturally Linda and I carefully read each incoming and outgoing message before it was actually transmitted. It would have been more difficult to read other people's mail if the other communications personnel were present. The UAR has established strong protections regarding individual privacy. But these were not normal times, and the "greater good" trumped legal and moral privacy concerns.

Additionally, we transmitted and received a continuous stream of navigational data to and from the asteroids en route to the moon's impact area. This high priority data was originated by our master navigation computer, which assigned a unique number to each incoming asteroid. We notified the retrieval crews of each asteroid's (meteor) arrival. Five minutes before impact, a klaxon would sound in the ore-processing area and a retrieval team would be dispatched by the shift supervisor. Each meteor tracking number was automatically transmitted to the supervisor's computer, who later recorded the type of ore and amount of content on his all-important production log. This was RAYCO's method of tracking production trends, mining and production costs, and estimating corporate profits and employee bonuses.

Linda and I went out of our way to meet the marines from first and second squads and all RAYCO employees. This accelerated activity level left us no time to spend with our own squad members. Gaining the confidence of the contractor's employees was a first step in determining whether Lieutenant Higgins had cleared out the traitors or if somebody remained inactive in a "sleeper" mode.

Jupiter Corporation operated each moon ship with three employees. In addition to Jupiter 1-C, they operated ships named 1-D and 1-E. Two of these moon ships were constantly in use with a third standing by on the moon at all times. Maintaining the third ship at our moon base was a safety precaution in case we had to evacuate the site. Jupiter flight personnel not out flying would normally keep to themselves. Fortunately, they were not suspected in the recent skirmish.

There were seventy-five RAYCO employees living and working at Moon Base Freedom. Thirty-five employees were assigned to the mining and manufacturing operations, while the remaining forty provided food service, greenhouse operations, medical care, and facility maintenance.

Negotiations were underway between Lieutenant Higgins and the on-site RAYCO manager to replace his eight employees who had attempted to sabotage our moon base. Needless to say, tensions were high and the lack of trust in all contractor employees was noticeable.

We also were alert to any marine who exhibited signs of emotional stress. I hated to think that one of us could turn on a fellow marine, but we had been taught not to take chances. The members of squad 1 were responsible for providing security to the power, sewage treatment, oxygen generation, and water treatment plants. Squad 2 was responsible for the contractors' quarters, ore processing, and manufacturing facilities. Each squad maintained half its personnel on guard duty while the other half was sleeping, eating, etc.

Linda asked, "Jim, have you thought about the possibility that people from another mining operation could have infiltrated our base?"

"Yes, that's a scary scenario, but we have to keep an open mind to all possibilities. I don't think he or she could stay for an indefinite time, but we should start checking the monitors and comparing faces to known identities, just in case. RAYCO contractors who didn't report strangers being present are equivalent to 'fifth columnists,' because with a workforce this small, nobody could hide among assigned staff without inside help."

"What's a fifth columnist?"

"It's an old term describing a subversive organization working within a country to give assistance to an invading enemy."

Monitors had been installed throughout the base and we controlled the monitors from the comm center. We'd installed a program on one of the computers that screened facial recognition features of all marines and Jupiter and RAYCO employees against images captured by the monitors. Linda and I installed warning devices at the monitoring station to alert us if a stranger appeared on the monitor. Additionally, Linda and I periodically and randomly repositioned each monitor's field of view to make it more difficult for someone to avoid being seen.

During dinner one evening, I joined one of the RAYCO contractors, introduced myself as a new arrival, and engaged him in conversation. His name was Steven Ames, a shift supervisor, who appeared eager to talk.

"Steve, since I'm new to the moon base, will you tell me about the mining operations?"

Steve appeared to relish this question, and between mouthfuls, he launched into a detailed explanation. "Precious metals abound in space. Although the moon contains some minor mineral deposits, they're buried under hundreds of feet of rock and dust. It's not economical to get those minerals today when you compare that to what's available in the asteroid belt."

"Why the asteroid belt and not Mars? After all, it is closer to earth."

"We discovered that the asteroid belt was easier to mine and asteroids contained minerals in much greater concentrations. Further, we could pick which asteroid we wanted! Harvesting asteroids became kinda like picking fruit from trees. If you want more apples, you pick apples. If you need pears, you pick pears.

"Why did you choose to stay on the moon?"

"Early mining corporations built large underground processing facilities on the moon. They created underground caverns using machinery similar to the tunnel-boring machines that dug under the English Channel and the Strait of Gibraltar. The cost of transporting these pieces of equipment from the earth was very expensive. After a detailed cost analysis, corporations determined the most economical solution was to build mining equipment on the moon. After some of these deposits were extracted, we used the ore to build our mining equipment. We then converted the caverns into a moon base and saved huge amounts of money."

"Steve, how did you save money by using the caverns?"

"By being able to use these caverns as our overall shelter, we don't have to worry about radiation, oxygen loss, or meteor strikes. Further, by using the rock as our primary walls and roof, we didn't have to rely on synthetic building materials.

"Today, large robotically controlled mining ships travel to the asteroid belt and look for asteroids containing precious metals. Nickel, iron, gold, and rare metals are highly prized finds. In addition, we get our water replenishment from space."

"What?"

"Yep, a frozen asteroid is periodically taken and sent to us where part of it is converted into oxygen and fuel for our rockets. We also take the balance of the water and send it to the treatment plant for processing. We don't take chances on introducing any unknown microorganisms that may be floating around in space!"

Steve took out a piece of paper and made a sketch similar to the following diagram:

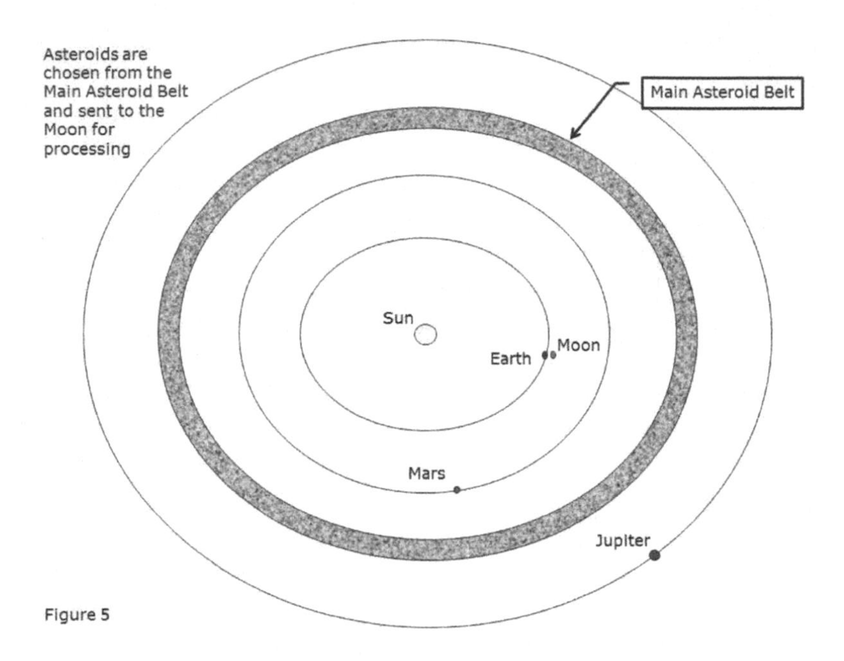

Figure 5

"Robots on the mining ship investigate an asteroid. If the asteroid checks out, they fire steel bolts into the asteroid and attach small rockets, fuel pods, and a coded navigational beacon. After using the mining ship to nudge the asteroid toward the moon, the rockets on the asteroid fire at prescribed intervals under the control of the navigational computer here at the moon base. The objective is to slowly bring the asteroid to our landing site on the moon's surface."

"Wow. That sounds like a tricky operation, and it brings up a lot of additional questions. For example, is the placement of the rockets on the asteroid critical?"

Steve grinned and said, "You bet, Jim. The rockets we use are not powerful and the asteroid must be guided down here from millions of miles away. We have learned that any asteroid weighing a hundred tons or more must have at least six rockets evenly spaced around its center of gravity. While there is some margin of error, the more accurate the placement, the less rocket fuel will be required. Also, if we give the asteroid a nudge from the ship, the rockets will have a much easier time because they will not have to waste fuel overcoming the asteroid's inertia."

"I'll bet that is a really precise nudge."

"Yeah, the timing, amount of thrust, and total burn time are controlled by the navigational computer located in the commo center. You see, each asteroid within the Asteroid Belt is moving at a slightly different speed. And our moon is rotating around Earth, which is also moving in a completely different orbit and speed from the asteroids. Combine those factors with the gravitational pull of the planetary bodies and the varying distances between each asteroid and the moon as it begins its journey. Hitting the impact area on the moon from the asteroid belt is kinda like shooting a pistol while jumping off a cliff and hitting the lettering on a baseball in midair from two miles away."

I was very impressed and said so.

Steve said, "Well, powerful computer programs constantly crunching vast yet accurate astral-navigational data make it all possible. That and reliable communications," he added.

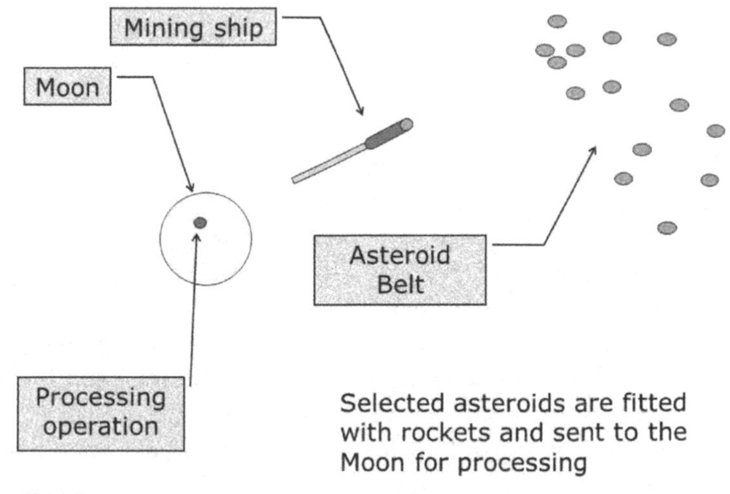

Figure 7

"Steve, how many rockets are carried by a mining ship?"

"They carry as many as possible. That's governed by take-off limitations placed on the mining ship. Even though objects weigh only one sixth as much on the moon as they would on Earth, we are still limited by total gross weight. Typically, we can send about fifteen hundred rockets and their fuel cells on each mining ship in addition to six robots."

"Why use six robots?"

"The six robots give us redundancy which translates into very high reliability, plus or minus three standard deviations from the mean. In layman's terms, we estimate that six robots give us a 99.73 percent probability of mission success. We can't afford to send a mining ship millions of miles away just to have a key piece of equipment fail its mission."

I already knew the answer to this question but asked it anyway. "How many ships does Jupiter Corporation operate?"

"Jupiter operates six autonomous mining ships. At any given time, Jupiter will have anywhere from seventy-five to one hundred fifty asteroids en route to the moon from the asteroid belt. If our mining ships stopped their operations tomorrow, we would still have meteors hitting the moon for about five months."

"How long does a mining ship stay out in the asteroid belt?"

"Until they've expended their asteroid booster rockets or until all robots become inactive. Usually two to three months of 'round-the-clock work. Our robots are preprogrammed to perform their tasks." Laughing, he added, "Naturally, the robots don't mind the overtime!"

"How do the robots know which asteroid is worth collecting?"

"They use an embedded software program and sophisticated but rugged analytical equipment which was developed over several years of expensive trial and error. That software program is one of our company's most closely guarded secrets."

"How long does it take to get to and from the asteroid belt?"

"Not thinking about leaving us, are you?" Steve grinned. "It takes about six months of steady burn to make the trip."

"If we have six ships, how many mining ships are operated by the competition?"

"Comtec and the European Union each have two mining ships. Transvaal operates five ships, and I've heard they're building two more."

"Do they individually control their navigation systems?"

"You betcha! Allowing a competitor control over your navigation system would be like giving a burglar the combination to your vault! All they would have to do is change the coordinates of the impact area and they could start harvesting your meteors."

"One final question: What is done with the waste from the meteor after processing?"

Steve said, "We carry the waste outside and dump it in the impact area each time we retrieve a meteor. Over the years, sections of our impact area have been built up a few meters from waste disposal."

"Hey, thanks for talking with me, Steve. You are a font of knowledge. I really appreciate your educating me about this fascinating topic."

"Anytime, Jim. After the recent problem, I think everyone here needs to make a special effort to get along and mend fences. By the way, some of the guys get together after third shift and play cards. I'd love to have you join us."

"Thanks, Steve. I'd love to play cards with you. Unfortunately, with the additional hours we're working, I don't know when I'll have time to join you."

The next ten days flew by. Neither Linda nor I were able to identify anything unusual out of the activities occurring at the base.

Then one evening I was on communications watch and began reviewing some incoming message traffic.

Voila! Hidden in a routine supply message from RAYCO back on Earth was some extraneous text at the end of the message.

```
SUPPLY MSG
DTG 081223511915Z

TO   RAYCO SUPPLY TECH, BASE CAMP FREEDOM

FROM   RAYCO SPACE SUPPLY DIVISION, MEMPHIS, TN, UAR

THE FOLLOWING PARTS WILL BE SHIPPED ON 08152351:
P/N                      NAME                      QTY
9245981257723402         BOARD CIRCUIT LEADER        4
WH44585222314            HARNESS LEADER              1

CONTAINER RAYCO-MBA-2351J489231

ES9WE LMCRT G43ES O81VR 7HWEC UVBQS MI63S UCXB4

BT
END
```

What does this mean?

Figure 8

The evenly spaced additional characters had no apparent meaning. That indicated that it was either transmission interference—or a coded message. I checked the logs and no mention of unusual atmospherics had occurred. This increased the probability that I had discovered a coded message.

There is a policy forbidding government contractors from sending encoded messages over the UAR Military Communication Network. Our communication network encodes all its messages prior to transmission. Contractors engaging in "double encoding" is against UAR Military Communication Network policy.

CHAPTER 20
Secret Messages

My first action was to note the name of the intended recipient. Unfortunately, there was no name, just the job title "supply technician." RAYCO had three supply technicians stationed at Base Camp Freedom. One of those three could be a subversive and we would need to carefully watch him or her. Our first problem would be in identifying the technician who'd received the hidden message.

I contacted Linda and called her into the communications center.

She arrived rubbing sleep from her eyes. "What's up, Jim?"

"Sorry to wake you, babe. I may have stumbled upon a hidden message."

That grabbed her attention.

Decoding encrypted messages is an art form. Messages have been encrypted for thousands of years. Various individuals have used different means of ciphering messages. They all had one thing in common: someone wanted to keep an enemy from reading the message, and the enemy discovering the message wanted to break the code and read its content. Over time, after huge amounts of money was spent and countless experiments were conducted, ciphering equipment became more sophisticated and deciphering equipment became more capable. It was nothing more than a race of one-upmanship, with power and advantage going to the winner.

We fed the extraneous traffic into our main computer and used every known programmed algorithm. After several hours of crunching numbers, letters, and special characters, I failed to notice any discernible pattern.

Linda took a turn and drew a blank too.

"Linda, maybe we're not dealing with any known code pattern. I'm thinking we may be looking at a one-time substitution code. I've searched through every e-book imaginable and none are being used as the code key. But what if one of the RAYCO employees smuggled in a printed book? With an unknown book available at this location, it would be virtually impossible for us to break the code and understand its contents. We need to begin a search for a book that may not appear on our master list. I also wonder if the book could be 'hidden in plain sight.'"

"After checking your procedures and undertaking some additional analyses, I agree that there could be another book being used. I'll visit the supply technicians' area and conduct a quick search." She leaned over, gave me a quick kiss on my cheek, and said, "Hold down the fort, sweetie."

While Linda was gone, I began searching previous messages for similar extraneous codes. Relying on the computer to search for abnormalities, I found three previous messages with extraneous characters. Interestingly, the first message was received just one week prior to the recent uprising during in four marines had been killed. The next two messages were received during the weeks that Lieutenant Higgins and First Sergeant Barnett were operating the communication center. I couldn't expect the leaders to catch the abnormal messages, but the commo team should have found the first message. It was an expensive oversight and one that had exacted a high price.

Linda returned about two hours later and flopped down in her chair. "I pilfered through their stuff—and nada. I couldn't find any book."

"Yeah, while you've been sniffing though other men's clothing, I found some interesting incoming traffic. It appears a total of four messages have been sent to our mystery person. One message was sent a week before the recent trouble and two more just prior to our arrival. They were all addressed to 'RAYCO Supply Tech.'"

My next step was to alert the Space Marines Intelligence Division and ask them to initiate an investigation at the message source within Jupiter Corporation. Even if the static did not contain any hidden message, my job was to alert intelligence division. They had more sophisticated equipment and could help Linda and me determine the exact content of the transmission.

"Jim, did you check on the outgoing messages?"

There was a pause when I realized the importance of what she'd said. I thought, *Man, how stupid can I get?*

"That's right—whoever sends out an encrypted message is likely the recipient of the incoming encrypted messages! And we have a means of finding out who authored the outgoing messages!" I quickly accessed the outgoing messages that were sent during the last four weeks and found nothing. "No outgoing messages contain similar extraneous code. This can only mean one of two things. Whoever is receiving the coded messages is answering them by another means of communication, or the replies are being sent disguised as plain text."

As I thought about this new wrinkle, Linda said, "Is it possible that the person receiving the coded message is taking the reply outside and leaving it for someone from another mining outfit?"

"You may be right. This could be a dead-letter operation. It'll be difficult to find the traitor. I mean you can't just go outside and wait for him or her to walk by."

"True, but we have a camera that will follow a heat signature, don't we? Why not install it outside?"

"Hey, I'll go. It's my turn to wander about anyway."

Linda rigged a camera with attachments and put it in a bag while I hurried to the barracks and put on my space suit.

"Be careful, darling."

I took the bag from her and entered the airlock. This was the first time I had been outside since our arrival.

It was twilight as I exited the air lock. The sun was over the moon's horizon but its rays cast eerie shadows. I didn't want to use a light so I hopped along in the dim light and began looking for the best location for our camera. It needed a clear view of both air locks and not be noticeable to people entering or leaving the facility. The best location given these constraints was above the moon base on the cliff face. Positioning the camera there would give an unrestricted view of anyone entering or leaving the moon base. I estimated the cliff to be about one hundred fifty feet high. Since I didn't have any climbing gear, I was forced to walk about a half mile before coming to a rock-filled chute that permitted me to scramble to the top of the ridge. I quickly hopped back to a place directly above the main entrance to the moon base and wasted no time attaching the camera to the cliff face.

As I straightened up and looked around, I noticed some additional tracks along the ridge directly above the mining entrance. I turned on my helmet light and began a quick search back of the edge. About ten feet from the edge of the cliff, I discovered a large metal bowl. It was roughly two feet across and painted a dark color. After lifting the bowl, I found a coil of thin nylon line. The line was staked to the top of the cliff by an embedded steel spike and the free end was tied to a brown plastic container measuring about six-by-twelve-by-one half inches thick. How simple! Our mole would wait until he or she received a message from the control and then write a response. Someone would notify the messenger to drop the plastic box over the cliff and wait for the written reply. It was almost foolproof. I couldn't wait to tell Linda. We would have to inform Lieutenant Higgins since we needed help neutralizing the traitor.

I photographed the items and replaced the bowl. I then took the camera bag, filled it with small rocks, and dragged it around the ground to hide my own footprints. That being done, I checked my oxygen level (it was getting low) and hurried back inside.

CHAPTER 21
The Message Box

During Rolf's final days on Earth, Mr. Leher informed him that Agent Schmidt had installed a message box on the cliff overlooking Moon Base Freedom. He further stated that Rolf's job was to place and retrieve messages from the box.

Rolf didn't like thinking of himself as a postman, so he decided someone else would be the messenger boy. After getting to know Pieter, Ibrahim, Hussein, Solly, and Shanna, Rolf knew he could trust them to follow his instructions. Selecting the person who could keep his or her mouth shut was another matter. The ideal candidate was Shanna, who had become emotionally attached and very loyal to Rolf.

The UAR moon base was about twelve miles from Transvaal Base. Rolf assigned himself a spare meteor retrieval vehicle, placed extra oxygen bottles aboard, got Shanna, and drove within a mile of the UAR facility.

Upon arrival, they switched to fresh oxygen bottles and walked the final mile to a point on the ridge directly above the moon base. Together they found the upended bowl. Shanna silently watched Rolf as he placed a message in the box and lowered it over the cliff. Rolf and Shanna returned to the vehicle and drove back to Transvaal Base.

Once inside, Rolf said, "Shanna, you must never tell anyone where we've gone or what we did. This will be our secret."

"You know I would never tell. But I don't understand why you took me along."

"Because you, my wonderful Shanna, will deliver the next message for me and will bring me any messages you find in the box. Do this and your reward will be great."

"You know I will help you willingly. I don't need a reward. Besides, I love being outside and seeing all the stars around us. It's so beautiful."

"Nevertheless, you will be rewarded, my love."

Shanna kissed Rolf and returned to her duties while Rolf paid a visit to the communication center.

Rolf composed and sent the following message:

> TO: Dieter Leher, Transvaal Corporate Headquarters, Department 5
> SUBJECT: Establishing Contact
> Have begun communication with Deep Six as directed. Request further guidance.
> Rolf
> End Transmission

Rolf smiled as he sent the message. He decided not to take any further action unless specifically directed by Mr. Leher. He thought, *I'll let the corporate bigwigs call the shots on this operation. No sense in sticking my neck out; especially since I know for a fact there will be no reward in it for me. In fact, I don't care if his plan succeeds or fails. I will do just enough to keep that idiot from activating the device planted in my body. Even he should know that you can't threaten a man and expect him to show initiative.*

CHAPTER 22
Planning the Operation

After returning to the barracks, Linda was waiting for me and helped me out of my suit. I hurriedly got out of my suit and installed fresh oxygen bottles before stowing it in the barracks. Never put your suit away without making sure you have full oxygen bottles! This had been drilled into us until it became second nature. Nobody would last even minutes outside without oxygen. Keeping the suit ready for use is one of the imperatives.

In the commo center I told Linda about mounting the camera and my discovery of the hidden line and message box. "This proves that messages are being transmitted to or from the moon base. Out next step is to decide what to do with this knowledge."

"Okay, let's figure out the best way to handle this. One, we don't want a repeat of what happened a few weeks ago. Losing marines is unacceptable. Two, we have to stop whatever it is the bad guys are planning. Three, we have to catch the guilty SOB inside this base and neutralize the threat."

"Baby, I couldn't have summarized it better. Maybe it's time to brief Lieutenant Higgins?"

A few minutes after paging Lieutenant Higgins, he entered the commo center and was briefed on what we had discovered. The picture of the drop box was a little dim but it clearly showed the cord and box. His first reaction was to send a team to remove the line and message box. However, he quickly thought better of that idea and decided the best course of action would be to trap the messenger and mole.

In order to make the trap work, the message containing the code would be released. It would be up to us to catch the mole before he or she could carry out the mission. We needed a trap that would give us the highest probability of success. We couldn't afford to lose this round!

"Lieutenant, we noticed that only one message preceded the attack on the commo center. Also, two additional messages were sent after the attack."

"What's your point, Hawkins?"

"Sir, we don't know if releasing this message will precipitate another action. Unless we can break the code, we don't know what will happen."

"Hawkins, I appreciate your caution, but we can't sit on the message indefinitely. Failing to release the message may alert the traitor that we are on to him. Inaction can lead to failure too. In any case, it's my decision to take this calculated risk."

Linda spoke up and said, "Aye, aye, sir. Private Hawkins was only providing you with potential outcomes."

I continued. "Sir, we're continuously monitoring the incoming message station in the mess hall. It's possible they're using a one-time cipher book to encode and decode messages. If we could get our hands on that book, we should be able to read all the messages that were sent to Moon Base Freedom."

"Okay, Hawkins, your point is noted. Let me know when a supply tech visits the message console. Have you reported this to your intelligence chief?"

"Yes, sir. Intelligence division has more computing capacity and may be able to help us decipher the message traffic."

"Good work, Marines. Keep me informed."

In unison, Linda and I replied, "*Aye, aye, sir.*"

Linda dedicated a camera overlooking the message console and set up facial recognition software to alert us when any of the supply techs visited the console.

Linda's next step was to call up and review the personnel files of the three supply techs.

Wanda Allen, thirty-five, from New Brunswick, Canada. She

completed a six-year stint in the army where she received training and experience in supply operations. After being discharged, Wanda was hired by RAYCO and spent five years working in one of their manufacturing plants. She applied for a vacancy on the moon and was selected for this high-paying job.

James Ballantine, forty-two, from Russellville, Kansas. Prior to working for RAYCO, he spent six years in the navy assigned to the supply corps. James worked at several RAYCO maintenance facilities before applying for a posting on Moon Base Freedom. He's married with two children. There was no information on his wife.

Jose Morales, thirty-eight, from Mexico City. Prior to working for RAYCO, he spent four years in the coast guard. Afterward he spent time working as a mechanic with a farming company and later transferred into the parts department of an equipment manufacturing company owned and operated by RAYCO. He applied for a supply technician position on Moon Base Freedom. He is married and has three children. His wife is a RAYCO employee working in Houston, Texas.

"Linda, each supply tech seems to have a clean work record with no mention of disciplinary or any other negative comment. Could it be that one of the supply techs is merely a cut out in the operation?"

"Oh, Jim, you do want to make things difficult, don't you? However, I see your point. The real bad ass could be someone else and the supply tech is innocently forwarding messages to the real traitor. To be on the safe side, I'll ask intelligence division on Earth to check out these three supply techs from top to bottom. I'd like to know if anybody has some unexplained income or personal hardship."

"There is one additional possibility. Maybe this stuff we intercepted is not meant to be an intelligible message. Maybe it is simply an alert that the message box outside the moon base has a letter for our traitor. In any case, identifying and tracking the supply tech has to be the first step."

She said, "No, the first step is for you to go back to the message drop and plant an infrared camera that will notify us when our visitor comes back to lower his message box."

"Okay, I'll set up another camera. But how do you know our visitor is a he?"

Linda quipped, "Oh, that's simple; a female would have covered her tracks."

CHAPTER 23
Waiting and Watching

The next evening I was on duty when Ballantine turned up at the incoming message station and printed out the message. After notifying Lieutenant Higgins, I closely monitored our cameras to see what happened next.

"Sir, Ballantine returned to his desk located in the manufacturing facility. I didn't notice him passing any information to another person. After Ballantine attached the message to a clipboard, he has kept himself busy moving parts. It looks like he's only doing routine stuff."

"Roger. Thanks."

A buzzer sounded in our commo center alerting me that someone was approaching the cliff face overlooking our base. I quickly moved to the monitor and saw an infrared image of someone removing the bowl and lowering the box over the cliff face. When he was done, he moved away from the infrared camera's view.

"Lieutenant, please come to the commo center."

After he arrived, I briefed him on what I had seen.

"Hawkins, let me know who handles the clipboard in the supply section. This may be the person who suits up and leaves the base. Also, monitor the outside camera and let me know when someone retrieves the message from the box. Barring any surprises, we'll have our traitor in custody and may be able to eliminate an unwelcome visitor."

When Linda arrived to relieve me, I briefed her on the latest, kissed her 'bye, and headed to a shower and much-needed sleep.

CHAPTER 24
Springing the Trap

Twelve hours went by and nothing happened. I had relieved Linda, finished my shift, and was about to fall asleep when Linda called me to report to the commo center.

As I arrived, Linda and Lieutenant Higgins were watching the camera attached to the cliff. We saw someone stop the meteor retrieval sled and walk toward the cliff face where the message box was located.

Hearing my approach, Linda said, "Jim, several people reviewed the clipboard. There was no way to positively identify the mole. However, we should be able to nab the guy who is visiting the message box."

Lieutenant Higgins called First Sergeant Barnett and said, "Top, I want you to arrest the person who is on meteor retrieval duty. He should be entering the air lock any minute. Bring him to the marine barracks and secure any paper he may be holding."

At that moment, we were alerted to someone near the top of the cliff. Sure enough, our visitor had returned to retrieve the message box. Lieutenant Higgins called Corporal Hammond and said, "Corporal Hammond, please notify your sniper team to take out our visitor."

Linda and I were looking at one another when Lieutenant Higgins said, "I sent a sniper team to position itself in the crew quarters of the stand-by moon ship. After being alerted, they will exit the air lock and take a position on top of the crew quarters. At that height, they should be able to clearly see our visitor."

I asked, "Who is on the sniper team, sir?"

Lieutenant Higgins said, "I selected privates Springer and Dupree based on Corporal Hammond's recommendation. I'm told that Springer is an expert long-range shooter and Dupree is highly qualified as a spotter. They should be able to bag the visitor. Sanchez, please route their transmissions to us here in the commo center."

"Aye, aye, sir."

Linda, Lieutenant Higgins, and I listened as Suzanne answered Corporal Hammond's radio call. "Roger, we see the bad guy. I don't see anyone with him. He is 2244 feet away with zero wind. Ron, whenever you are ready."

A few moments later: "Corporal Hammond, Springer tagged the bad guy. He is down and not moving. We are going to investigate. We will call you when we get to the target; Dupree out."

Thirty minutes later, Dupree called and said, "Corporal Hammond, we have our bad guy. There is only one name on the suit. It says, 'Shanna.' Don't know if that is a first or last name. What should we do with the corpse?"

Lieutenant Higgins responded, "Private Dupree, this is Lieutenant Higgins. Lower the body to the bottom of the cliff. I will get First Sergeant Barnett to collect it. You and Springer did us proud. Come on in."

Lieutenant Higgins then called First Sergeant Barnett. "First Sergeant, please retrieve a body at the base of the cliff and have it brought to the infirmary."

"Wilco."

CHAPTER 25
Clean-Up

Lieutenant Higgins met First Sergeant Barnett in the marine barracks. "Okay, First Sergeant, who is our mole?"

"Lieutenant, you're not going to like this." First Sergeant Barnett stepped aside and revealed a corpse lying on a gurney. "Sir, he took something before we could stop him and it worked real fast. I couldn't get him to say anything before he lost consciousness."

"Who is he? I've seen him around but can't recall his name."

"His name is Tommy Nelson, one of the maintenance workers assigned retrieval duty this evening."

Lieutenant Higgins turned around and saw Steve Ames, the RAYCO shift supervisor standing in the doorway. "Come in, Steve. Tell me about Tommy Nelson."

Steve slowly entered the room. He was visibly shaken when he responded. "Lieutenant, Tommy has been on the moon base for about eight months. I've talked with him numerous times and played poker with him frequently. He was a quiet guy, very friendly and a hard worker. He never gave me a minute's trouble. In fact, there was absolutely nothing remarkable about him. He was not involved in the recent shooting, either. I have no idea why or how he became mixed up in these events."

"Thanks, Steve. After an autopsy is performed, I'll release the body into your custody."

"First Sergeant, did you get any papers off his body?"

"Yes, sir. Here's an envelope Tommy was carrying when we took him into custody."

"Thank you. I'll get this secured and analyzed. Maybe it'll tell us what's going on."

"First Sergeant, I believe our greatest danger is over. Please return the men to the regular duty roster."

"Aye, aye, sir!"

"Okay, let's take a look at the body named Shanna that Dupree and Springer bagged."

CHAPTER 26
A Crazy Plan

I received a transmission from intelligence division informing me that the disc sent for analysis contained a set of instructions that would have enabled Transvaal to gain control over our remote mining ships. Had the disc been uploaded into our navigation computer's memory, Moon Base Freedom would have become worthless until new mining ships were built and launched.

A crazy idea occurred to me. Time was against getting approval because it had to be implemented immediately for it to work. I established some trajectory parameters and input the data into our navigation computer. After a few minutes of crunching numbers, the data was downloaded onto a disc similar to the one we'd captured from the saboteur. My next job was to quietly suit up and go find the vehicle that had transported Shanna to our facility.

Once on the cliff, it was easy backtracking Shanna's footsteps. I quickly located her extraction vehicle and uploaded the contents of the disc into its onboard navigational computer. Being careful to leave everything as it was, I scuffed my footsteps around the vehicle and returned to base with a big smile while thinking of what I had set in motion.

CHAPTER 27
Answers, Please

On Transvaal Base, Rolf was summoned into Mr. Heinriks's office.

Mr. Heinriks asked Rolf, "Where's Shanna? She was supposed to report for kitchen duty more than one hour ago. Someone told me that two days ago, you and she left the base together and were gone more than four hours. Tell me if you know anything about her leaving today."

"Yes, Shanna and I did leave Transvaal Base. We had a reconnaissance mission to perform. And yes, she left for another mission today. I am aware that she is late returning, and I am worried about her."

"Rolf, when you arrived at this base, I gave you two directives. One, keep me informed of anything that will have an impact on my mining operations; and two, do not put my personnel or base in danger. Do you remember these directives?"

"Of course I do."

"Then please tell me why I received a message from the site manager at the UAR base a few minutes ago informing me that one of my workers has been shot for trespassing and attempted sabotage?"

This unexpected news stunned Rolf. He was having difficulty making himself think. The operation had seemed so simple. All Shanna had to do was deliver a message to a drop box!

Mr. Heinriks continued. "Shanna was a good worker. Her

absence will add work to the cooking staff, which will have an impact on my mining operations. Her being caught spying at the UAR moon base is putting my base in danger!

"Rolf, I have been supervising men for more than twenty years. I have learned to spot winners and losers in an instant. It is my belief that you are a loser. Always trying shortcuts and getting others to do your dirty work. It's no wonder you were demoted and sent away from corporate headquarters. And don't look so surprised. I have my information sources too.

"Well, I've got a new assignment for you, Rolf. You are personally going to the UAR moon base to retrieve Shanna's body. They are performing an autopsy before releasing her. After the body is released, you will drive over and collect her remains. I will have a worker accompany you to bring her vehicle back.

"If you have no questions, you may go."

Later that week, Rolf was notified to collect Shanna's remains. Mr. Heinriks met Rolf at the air lock and said, "My advice is to keep your mouth shut when you are in their facility. Just load the body onto the vehicle and get back."

As Rolf was returning with Shanna's body, he received a radio call from Transvaal Base. "Rolf, this is Mr. Heinriks. After you left this morning, I placed a call to Mr. Leher. I have him on the radio now. He wishes to speak with you. Gentlemen, please remember that you will have a two-minute transmission delay between responses."

"Rolf, are you there?"

"Yes, I'm here Mr. Leher."

"Rolf, what happened to our agreement? I gave you a simple task to perform and you didn't even try. Instead, you talked one of your coworkers into doing it for you. On top of that, you have alerted the UAR to our plans. It's good that you were not here in the board room when Mr. Von Stubben was informed of your latest failure. Rolf, you know what this means."

"Please, Mr. Leher. It wasn't my fault!"

"Now you have cost me a bet I made with your old boss, Mr. Ainsley. He bet me that you would refuse to accept responsibility for your errors."

"Wait! Mr. Leher, I fully acknowledge that I made a mistake. I should have delivered the message myself instead of sending someone else. However, I would have been shot doing this same job."

"You're forgetting one thing. You knew there was some danger in this assignment. You would have been more careful and would have avoided being detected. I'm sure the person you conned into delivering the message was unaware of any potential danger."

"Please, Mr. Leher. I know I can become your best agent. I'll do anything you ask. Just give me a chance to prove it."

"Oh, Rolf, I believe you're finally serious about your new job! You're really making my day. It's a good thing I've been recording this transmission. Nobody in the corporate office would believe you have changed so much!"

"Thank you, Mr. Leher. I promise I won't disappoint you ever again."

"I know you won't disappoint me again. Tell me, Rolf, is it beautiful where you are?"

"Mr. Leher, why are you asking that question? Please, Mr. Leher, don't ..."

CHAPTER 28
Payback

Two days later a maintenance technician at Transvaal Base accessed the onboard computer in Shanna's vehicle in order to update its navigational program. Data that Hawkins had added to the navigational computer was transferred to the Transvaal mainframe computer. From there, a set of instructions was transmitted to one of their remote mining ships.

Six hours later a Transvaal mining ship nudged an asteroid away from the asteroid belt and shoved it along a set of very precise coordinates.

Thirteen months later, Jim Hawkins and his wife, Linda, had completed their tour of duty at Moon Base Freedom. They were in their apartment in Washington DC watching television when a news flash scrolled across the screen.

> Johannesburg has been struck by an asteroid! The death toll is unknown but tens of thousands are feared dead and property damage is estimated in the billions of dollars. Outpourings of grief and sympathy are arriving from every country and mega-corporation throughout the world.

Jim slowly nodded while thinking, *Payback's a bitch.*

About the Author

Joe R. East Jr. served four years in the air force as a communications intelligence specialist. He again served his country by working as a civilian for the US Army. His thirty-six-year civil service career was primarily spent writing technical publications and teaching courses in logistics, program management, and contracting to soldiers and civilians. He has a bachelor's degree from Mississippi State University and a master's degree from Florida Institute of Technology.

Joe lives in Madison, Alabama, with his wife, Joan, and a dachshund, Socrates. Joe's favorite pastimes include golf, woodworking, skiing, singing, and reading. This is his first novel.